COLE SHOOT

D1519681

ALSO BY MICHEAL MAXWELL

The Cole Sage Mysteries

Diamonds and Cole
Cellar Full of Cole
Helix of Cole
Cole Dust
Cole Shoot

Three Nails
The Time Pedaler (with Tally Scully)

COLE SHOOT

A Cole Sage Mystery

MICHEAL MAXWELL

COLE SHOOT

ONE

Cole Sage leaned his bicycle against the wall of Kelly Mitchell's house boat and gave the heavy leaded-glass front door a rat-a-tat-tat. The door flew open and a clearly frantic Kelly waved Cole inside.

"I'm not ready!" Kelly said, batting at the cuffs of her jeans. "Look at this mess!"

From the knees down Kelly's jeans were coated in a white powdery substance.

"What is all that?" Cole inquired.

"The stuff out of the fire extinguisher!" Kelly huffed.

"You had a fire?" Cole said with a panicked look toward the kitchen.

"No, no we had a stupid safety class. And the hose on the fire extinguisher slipped out of my hand and I shot it all over my legs."

"A safety class?"

"Twice a year everybody on the dock does a safety review kind of thingy to make sure we know what to do in an emergency." Kelly stood and gave a sigh, "I'm sorry, Cole, I have to change. I'll only be a minute."

The unmistakable strains of *Anchors Aweigh* shattered the silence. "Hello." Kelly tried to sound chipper as she answered her cell phone. "We we're just leaving. No, we didn't forget you. I have no idea why Cole doesn't answer his cell phone." Kelly threw her hand out palm up at Cole, a clear sign of her irritation and want of an explanation.

Cole patted his front pockets and shrugged his shoulders.

"Okay," Kelly gave a big silent sigh. "We'll be right there." She snapped the phone shut. "Chris. Wondering where we were. Really Cole, I am in no mood for any of his drama."

"I'm sorry. I just thought it would be a nice gesture to give him a ride to the parade. Where do you suppose I left my phone?"

"Any of a thousand and one places," Kelly offered, as she made her way up the spiral stairs leading to the bedroom. "How is it that we are giving your boss's boyfriend a ride to the parade?"

"Chris doesn't drive. Chuck knew we were going and asked if we could give him a lift."

Setting in the middle of the floor, a dust covered pair of red tennis shoes called for attention. Cole scooped them up and took them outside to the side deck. He repeatedly slapped the soles together a let the wind blow the fire extinguisher's combination of baking soda and ammonium phosphate out across the water. Not quite as bright as they were before, but no longer coated in white. He laid the shoes just inside the door as he heard Kelly making her way back to the stairs.

"That's better," Cole smiled as Kelly came down the stairs in a pair of tight black jeans, a white silk blouse that buttoned up the side, and a pair of fiery red shoes with extremely pointed toes. Tied around her waist was a red and gold braided cord.

At the bottom of the stairs, Kelly pulled at the back of her blouse. "Sorry for the less-than-sparkling greeting."

"It sparkled all right," Cole teased.

With a sweeping, almost choreographed flair, Kelly slipped her arm through the strap of the gold lame bag that was looped over the banister and spun across the five feet to where Cole stood and gave him a kiss. "Let's go!" She said with a beaming smile and handed Cole the keys to her car.

Try as he may, Cole could not get used to the stealth mode silence of Kelly's new hybrid Toyota Prius. Twice he tried to restart the car at a stop signal. He had to admit, though, the dash screen that registered the fifty plus miles per gallon fuel consumption was impressive. He loved how he found himself going for block after block without ever hearing the combustion engine kick in.

As they made their way across the Golden Gate Bridge, Cole reached over and took Kelly's hand. The simple gesture was met with a gentle squeeze. That and the silence inside the car and the hum of the bridge seemed to bring peace to the manic frenzy that met Cole at the door. Moving through traffic and delighting in each other's company gave the glorious seventh day of February an added luster.

To Cole's amazement, the space directly in front of Chuck and Chris' house was unoccupied. The Prius slipped into the space and silently came to rest.

"I'll wait here."

"Be right back then," Cole said turning off the engine.

The door flew open just as Cole raised his knuckles to knock out his arrival. Standing in the doorway like a miscast character from a low budget, Hong Kong kung fu movie, stood Chris Ramos in a pair of red and black silk embroidered pajamas. He gave a deep bow.

"Gung Hay Fat Choy!" Chris fairly burst with enthusiasm.

"La Choy Chicken Chow Mein to you, too," Cole said, taking in the sight of Chris's outfit. On his feet were flat soled black silk slippers with golden dragons on the toes. Atop his head set a red skull cap with a black tassel and in his hands a pair of black tennis shoes with big red sparkling stars on the toes.

"For the Dragon Dance," Chris offered, seeing Cole eye the tennis shoes.

The memory of his mother, dressed for a costume party, came into Cole's mind. He couldn't have been more than twelve years old at the time; but he remembered clearly her shiny black silk kimono, courtesy of a neighbor's plundering after the war. A huge, golden dragon covered most of the back. She sprayed her hair jet black and it was pulled back and held in place with a pair of lacquered chop sticks. She powdered her face with some kind of white make up and painted her lips with a very small, bright red, exaggerated bee sting lip shape. Never one to wear much make up at all, this costume and Asian make-over came as a real shock to Cole. The thing that he remembered most, though, was the black eye liner she had applied to give her eyes a distinctive almond shape, changing his very-blonde Anglo mother into a Geisha for the night.

"So, no eye make-up to make the illusion complete?" Cole quizzed.

"I will not play into cruel racial stereotypes," Chris snapped.

"And red pajamas and little tasseled yarmulke isn't?"

"This is a tribute, not a parody," Chris said, holding his chin in an exaggerated incline.

"Of course," Cole just stared. His mind jumped from idea to idea and the rapid fire neurons made enough synaptic connections to land fully formed on the platform of twenty-first century political correctness. *Were Asians as offended by Charlie Chan and John Wayne's Attila the Hun, in The Conqueror, as African Americans are at someone in blackface?* Cole just nodded his head.

"Is there more to this outfit or are you ready to go?"

"I am ready for the dragon! The question is, is the dragon ready for me?" Chris pulled the door closed and pranced down the steps to the sidewalk.

"Love your blouse, Kelly," Chris said, sliding into the back seat.

"It's been in the closet for ages. I never seem to remember it when I need it."

"I'm glad it came out," Chris giggled. "Love the neckline. Of course you have such a lovely neck anyway," Chris gushed.

"Where did you get those pajamas? They are gorgeous."

"You don't think they're too much?"

"For a Chinese New Year's celebration? Never!"

"Tomorrow they are yours!"

"Oh I couldn't, they must be terribly expensive."

"I think you would be simply outrageous in them!" Chris giggled.

"Girls, girls! If we can suspend the fashion Diva patter long enough to tell me where we are supposed to drop you off, Chris, it would be wonderful."

"Just because you're dressed like some butch, lumberjack wanna be, you don't have to be nasty. What's up with Mr. Poopy Party, anyway?"

"Sorry, but you did say ten o'clock. It is now nine forty-five."

"That's better. I do appreciate the ride, but your tone, my goodness."

"Okay, okay. Where are we dropping you?" Cole said, looking in the rear view mirror.

"Chinatown Community Center on Larkin and Pine. We meet there."

"How is it that *you*, pardon the obvious, a non-Chinese, was asked to be part of the News Year's Dragon Dance?" Cole asked, pulling into traffic.

"Tommy Fong, who I did some design work with, is the brother of the "Year of the Rat Celebration" committee chairman. I said how much I loved the Dragon Dance, and how I would love to be part of the dragon, and he offered to get me a spot. If you were nicer to people you could have nice things happen to you, too."

"Like spending the afternoon with my nose in somebody's butt?

"Ah, but you're on the receiving end too!' Chris giggled.

Kelly rolled her eyes and said, "Boys, Boys can we just ride along in peace?"

Chris folded his arms and sat with a broad grin on his face, delighted with having the last word. The banter was the best part of their friendship, and it was the struggle to get the best and last word in with Cole, that he cherished most.

As they turned onto Larkin, Chris leaned forward and thrust the tennis shoes between the seats. "Look for my twinkle toes and you'll know which legs on the dragon are me. Chuck can't make it so you guys are my rooting section. "

"We'll be at the Great Wall later if you want to join us," Kelly offered.

"Thanks, but the dragon crew is having a banquet after the parade. I really do appreciate the ride."

"Kelly, you got the bag of marbles?" Cole asked.

"Marbles?" Kelly asked with no clue of Cole's meaning.

"To throw under the dragon."

"Stop," Kelly said in mock disgust. "We'll be about half way along the parade route. You probably can't see out, but we'll be yelling for you."

"Here we go," Cole said rolling to a stop.

"Thanks for the ride, you guys. Anybody got a camera? I'd love a picture of my feet peeking out from under the dragon."

"Just the one on the phone."

"That will have to do! Love you, bye!" Chris chirped, bouncing from the car. As he stepped from the street to the curb, he turned and waved.

"You've got to admit with all his quirks, drama, and hyper activity, he's quite charming."

"Never," Cole said waving back at Chris.

"Do you two ever not squabble?" Kelly asked, hoping for a serious answer.

"Never," Cole chuckled and made a right hand turn to begin the search for a place to park.

By noon, the wind died down and the sun was like a warm cozy quilt as Cole and Kelly made their way to the parade route. People seemed to be streaming in from everywhere. Police on motorcycles and horses patrolled the streets. Patrolmen on foot stood at intersections in a futile attempt to keep the traffic moving. Barriers and patrol cars blocked side streets and soon the sidewalks were nearly solid with people jockeying for a spot with a clear view of the parade.

Cole decided on a corner spot near Kearny and Washington, right in front of a satellite TV store. It was just far enough away from the reviewing stand and the more tourist-centered areas for the crowds to have thinned down some. The big green awning in front of the store would be just enough to keep the sun out of their eyes, but still keep them on the warm side of the street. Even though it was near the end of the parade route, Cole figured it was a good spot because the parade turned the corner heading for Columbus and the end of the route.

Kelly had a habit of keeping two folding chairs in the back of the car. She loved being able to have impromptu picnics with a view, and Cole loved not having to sit on the ground. With chairs unfolded and a box lunch from Nanking Restaurant on their lap, Cole and Kelly chatted and chewed away the hour before the parade would pass their location.

Always one to be prepared, Kelly was armed with an official guide to Chinese New Year she picked up from the Chinatown Merchants Association office weeks before the parade. To Cole's delight, she acted as his official commentator, sprinkling facts and figures from her guide book, as the first of the over one hundred entries in the parade began to pass in review.

"The Chinese New Year's parade has been celebrated in San Francisco since the time of the Gold Rush and is a treasured part of the heritage of the city," Cole said in his best news anchor baritone. Knowing Kelly's fondness for researching anything they went to, Cole did some homework of his own and would try and out-factoid Kelly's commentary.

"We are really good at this!" Kelly bubbled, "We should be on TV."

"You maybe, but I have a face strictly for radio," Cole returned.

The color, noise, and excitement of the parade were a stunning complement to the clear, blue sky and gentle breeze that embraced the city. Bands, acrobats, and floats with members of San Francisco's Chinese Opera all passed by, each seeming more beautiful and elaborate than the last. Firecrackers accented the festivities with barks, sparks, and crackling that made children squeal and adults throw their hands up over their ears. The smoke and smell of gunpowder and sulfur swirled and drifted through the crowd. Civic groups tossed candy and offered flags and streamers to the people lining the streets. Applause and laughter, cheers and the banging of gongs and cymbals greeted each new section of the parade.

An hour into the celebration Cole stood to stretch his legs.

"I'll be back in a minute. I need to stretch my legs."

"I'll be here." Kelly gave him a bright smile.

As he made his way up the street Cole took in the sight of the hundreds of jubilant spectators filling the sidewalks. He watched as a large group of people overflowed into the street like water coming over the top of a dam. The crowd seemed to move like a wave and the tone of the noise coming from their direction changed and intensified.

Cole walked a bit further, but was stopped by the congestion. People began to move from the sidewalk to the street. A dozen or more tried to cross, dodging and cutting through the startled lines of a marching band. Cole was distracted by the sound of a man yelling behind him.

As he turned, Cole saw an Asian man cursing and yelling as he rose to his knees, "What the hell!"

In an instant, two Latinos dressed in red t-shirts and baseball caps stepped into the street and began punching and kicking the man. A woman in a red and gold embroidered Chinese dress stepped from the crowd and began screaming. She tried to intercede on behalf of the man who was struggling to guard against the brutal onslaught of the attack. She grabbed one of the attacker's arms. He spun about and, with a fierce combination of punches, drove the woman to the ground. Within seconds, it was over and the two assailants disappeared back into the crowd.

Several onlookers rushed to the aid of the woman. The noise of an approaching marching band drowned out much of the noise of the crowd, but the mood and posture of the people on the street had changed. In just moments, the waving of flags and streamers ceased. The faces of the people went from eager anticipation for the next participants in the procession, to the fear of the scene around and behind them.

Across the street to Cole's left, the source of the first disturbance stepped off the curb and into the street. He tried to count the number of young Asian men who suddenly broke from the spectators. His view was blocked by a troop of acrobats. His best guess was ten to twelve, but the number seemed to shift and flow as they slipped in and out of his vision.

It was obvious from their dress that these young men were part of a street gang too. They wore crisp, starched, long white t-shirts that hung nearly to their knees. Along with baggy khaki work pants, they wore snowy-white baseball caps with a black and silver **FCBZ** embroidered on the front. The Fire Cracker Boyz were an up-and-coming Chinese street gang Cole had read about. Most of their arms were heavily tattooed and they all wore long silver chains around their necks. Their presence, and the increased Chinatown violence of the last several months, made them an unwelcome site at the parade.

A defensive sense of urgency came over Cole as he began moving back toward Kelly.

"Look Cole, here it comes," Kelly called out.

Fifty yards up the street, the crimson Dragon snaked its way toward them. From sidewalk to sidewalk, slithering along, writhing, and rippling like a wave. Fire crackers popped by the hundreds and a bluish cloud fogged the street. Smoke puffed from the cavernous mouth as the head snapped and roared at the cheering throngs lining the street.

The FCBZ crew stood at a sloppy version of "attention", their arms behind their backs, only a few yards up from where Kelly stood watching the dragon. As Cole watched, a large group of red clad Latinos moved in front of Kelly. For a moment, she disappeared from his view.

"Kelly!" Cole yelled trying to get her attention above the roar of the crowd.

The red mass moved past him and Cole was jostled as they roughly made their way up the street.

"Kelly!" Cole waved his arms again, trying to get her attention.

"Look!" she called back, pointing at the dragon quickly approaching them.

"Get your stuff together. We need to get out of here. There's going to be trouble," Cole said as he reached where she stood. But it was too late.

The rapid fire of multiple gunshots seemed to add a separate soundtrack to the parade. The two gangs of young men moved through the crowd in the slow motion images of the mind's inability to accept what it knows is true.

People ran in all directions, sending the spectators into each other, pushing, shoving, and trampling anyone who got in the way. The dragon stopped moving momentarily when the head collided with the tail. As the crimson tube attempted to straighten, several pairs of feet stumbled as it moved directly between the two gangs of shooters.

A small group of dots expanded into bloody splotches on the snowy-white shirt front of an FCBZ member as he dropped to the ground. Before Cole could take a breath, a stray bullet struck the forehead of a dark haired women who froze in terror as the gunfire erupted. The wall behind Kelly zinged with the sound of a bullet deflecting off a piece of metal trim.

Cole instinctively pulled Kelly to the ground and covered her with his body. The pop, pop, pop of small caliber pistols, and the thunderous blast of large bore, automatic handguns echoed in the street as the shooting continued. Cole could feel Kelly's heavy breathing beneath him as he tried to get a visual of the shooters faces.

I must to be able to describe facial features, outstanding characteristics, and individual tattoos Cole thought as the shots suddenly stopped. Just as quickly, the slow motion snapped back into real time. The crowd pushed, shoved, and tried to run both ways up the street.

"Are you OK?" Cole asked gently, as he rolled and stood, offering Kelly his hand.

"Yes, I'm fine. What's happening, Cole?" She panted.

"Gang shoot-out! Get back!" Cole pressed Kelly against the wall with the back of his arm. The crowd pushed and stumbled past them, knocking their ice chests and folding chairs into the street.

In one hysterical moment, the parade was shattered. The marching band broke formation, and like a colorful, chaotic mob they scattered through the spectators. Within sixty seconds the block was nearly deserted.

Somewhere into the madness, both gangs disappeared. Six lifeless bodies lay sprawled and twisted on the sidewalk. Legs and arms dangled into the gutter, bodies draped across the curb, the dead and dying lying in puddles of crimson. Moaning and crying replaced the joyous sounds of the parade as several small groups of people knelt, and stood around men, women, and children hit by stray bullets.

In the center of the street, the dragon lay collapsed in an oddly snarled heap; the head broken off at the neck, eyes skyward, mouth gaping open, a faint wisp of smoke escaping from one of the eyes. Sticking out from under the torn and broken dragon was a pair of black tennis shoes, one pointing up and one twisted to the side, exposing a red star.

"Kelly, I think you need to stay here."

Cole moved quickly toward the dragon, his eyes never leaving the red star. A hundred things flew through his mind as he made his way across the street. He was too much the realist not to know who he would find; his concern was *what* he would find.

For a brief moment, Cole stood next to the dragon. Several feet to his left, he heard a groan, but nothing in front of him. Grasping two of the bamboo support ribs, Cole gently lifted the torn silk form.

Chris Ramos lay with his arms over his head, his hands clutching his elbows. A large, dark stain covered the front of his red silk shirt, a look of complete and utter disappointment on his face. There was no life in his eyes.

TWO

Weather is a strange thing. In the course of three days, snow can melt, a drought can end, or in the case of San Francisco, sunshine and blue skies can turn to fog. The grey veil of fog that shrouded the city the morning of Chris Ramos' funeral seemed a final insult to a man whose life had been one of torment for what he was, and a well spring of joy for those who really knew him for who he was.

The small chapel at St. Bartholomew's had to be abandoned for the cavernous main sanctuary of the cathedral. An hour and a half before the service was to begin, the chapel was full and several hundred people were lined up outside. Father Martinez directed his staff like a crazed orchestra director. Within minutes the cathedral doors were opened, the alter vessels and flowers were all in place, looking like it was the original plan.

Chuck Waddle, Carlos' long-time partner and Cole's boss, asked Cole to be a pallbearer. As a rule, Cole Sage did not go to funerals. Ellie's marked an end to the twenty-odd years he successfully avoided almost all end of life ceremonies.

Cole stood outside the church near the hearse. The five other pallbearers were a combination of friends, relatives, and business associates of Chris' and all strangers to Cole. As he waited silently, his mind wandered back to the day he first acted as a pallbearer. It was June 12, 1968 and Cole, the high school kid, faced death for the first time. Carol Anne Wilkins was a classmate and family friend. Her parents came to the Sage home, and, through tears and kind words, asked Cole to be a pallbearer. As a small boy, he attended services for one of his grandparents; but the memory was just a blur. Cole had no idea what a pallbearer was, but he felt the importance of the position and agreed.

Cole's mother took him to buy a suit. It was dark, navy blue with embossed metal buttons and wide lapels. A snow-white shirt, so crisp and starchy it actually made a crackling sound when he tried it on, was added to the ensemble. Most of all, he remembered his mother turning to him and telling him to go pick out a tie.

His first choice was a flaxen, paisley belly warmer, a swirling floral affair with burgundy thistles that caught Cole's eye and would be the envy of all his peers. His knowing nothing about color or propriety made for an instant rejection of Cole's choice and his mother accompanied him to the rack for a second attempt. The hippie influenced width was acceptable but it must be dark muted colors to match the suit. Cole found the same paisley print in blue, a compromise that was easily reached.

Cole smiled at his memory as another man joined the group waiting in front of the cathedral. He easily rolled back to 1968 and the day he waited in front of the church where Carol's funeral was held, as he stood silently in his new suit. The sharp pain and shock of Robbie Montebello's words hit Cole afresh.

"I sure hope it's not heavy," Robbie had whispered.

"What?" Cole replied.

"The casket. My dad said sometimes they are really heavy."

At that moment, the hearse rolled up in front of the church and Cole could see the white coffin in the back. A blanket of white chrysanthemums covered the box inside. Like a gust of bitter wind, Cole realized Carol was in the coffin. 'Pallbearer' was just a nice way to say he would be carrying a box with his dead friend in it. Cole began to cry.

The voice of the man next to him interrupted Cole's thoughts.

"See that guy?" the man indicated a skeletally thin man who stood smoking and crying. "He sees the handwriting on the wall." The stout Hispanic man to the left of Cole blew smoke and looked at him for the first time.

"How's that?" Cole answered.

"AIDS. He's been fighting it for years. Sad, he's a good guy. I'm Rick, Chris' cousin," He said offering his hand.

"Cole Sage."

"The newspaper guy."

"That's me."

"They're not going to catch the punks who killed Chrissie are they?" Rick's voice lost the friendly tone as he crushed out his cigarette on the sidewalk. "They'll get away with it. Cops are afraid of them."

Before Cole could respond, an ashen-pale funeral director in a Bible-black suit addressed the six men standing by the hearse. "Gentlemen, the mourners have all been seated and now it is our responsibility to carry the deceased to the vestibule."

"Chris. His name was Chris," Rick's voice cracked with emotion as he corrected the pale man.

"Yes, Chris." The funeral director gave his shoulders a jerk backward and began speaking in a soft, deliberate voice. "We will join Father Martinez in the back of the church. He will drape the casket with the pall, do the introductory blessing, and then you will each take your spot on the rail and roll the trolley to the altar. Once there, roll the trolley so the casket is parallel with the altar. At that point, please take the seats under the arch to the right of the altar. There is a sign reading "Reserved" across the front row. At the end of the Mass, the process is reversed and we will lift the casket from the trolley and return it to the hearse. Any questions?"

No one responded. The men silently approached the back of the hearse. The Funeral director pulled out the rolling tray on which the snow-white and gold-trimmed casket sat. Just like Carol's Cole thought. The pallbearers, without direction or speaking, each took one of the six handles and in one swift, smooth motion removed the casket. With almost fluid movement, the six men made their way up the twelve steps to the front doors of the cathedral. Without hesitation, they set it gently on the waiting black draped trolley.

The journey to the altar was a blur to Cole, an ocean of heads and black clothes. The smell wafting from the ocean of flowers, mixed with the pungent sweet odor of the priest's incense burner, made Cole slightly lightheaded.

As he took his seat with the other pallbearers, he saw Kelly sitting near the aisle several rows from the front. She was dressed in a black jacket, turtleneck, a small black hat, and sunglasses. Cole was taken by the beauty of her profile. I'll just try to focus on her he thought, as he settled into his seat.

Chuck Waddle sat, head bowed, his wide shoulders heaving, his rugged suntanned hands covering his face. The rough, hard drinking, Eastwoodesque editor looked frail and defeated as he sat weeping alone on the front pew.

The church was filled with a large contingency of Hispanic men and women, Southeast Asians, and Artsy types that Chris worked with in the design industry. Conspicuous in dress and size, three rows of elegantly quaffed and hatted drag queens turned out to pay their last respects to one of their great fans. Black sequins and boas seemed somehow the most sincere tribute to the flamboyant little man in the showy white coffin.

In the midst of the boas and sequins, stood Chris's favorite drag queen. He stood because he was a dwarf. Cole only met the little African American man once. He had come to Chuck and Chris's house for a fitting. Chris Ramos' love for flashy outfits spilled over into his love of drag performance, making him the go-to-guy for outrageous stage outfits. Franklin Jackson, or "Biggie Smallie", as he was known on stage, was being outfitted in a gold lame jumpsuit that looked like a cross between Elvis and the Funkadelics. Cole recalled Biggie sticking out his ample rump in Cole's direction and saying in his most femme voice, "Does this make my butt look big?" He was a hilarious little guy and the rapid fire exchanges with Chris could have been show stopping stage patter. Cole would miss his friend's laser wit and his mind's warp speed processing. So would Franklin Jackson, as was evident by his red eyes, tear streaked cheeks, and gold lame cape.

The sound of the priest's voice faded as Cole sank deep into his own thoughts. Like a swirling Technicolor dream, his mind lapsed into rotating images of Chris in a montage of his exotic, over the top outfits. A holiday-centric mix of costumes clashed with the images of the Chinese New Year's Parade; bloody bodies, screaming, panicked parents with children in their arms, spliced together with Chris opening the door and grinning in his red pajama parade outfit. Like Dorothy's house crashing in Oz, it all landed, exposing only the red sequined star tennis shoes of the body sprawled beneath the dragon.

Cole turned his focus back to Kelly. As the priest spoke of unconditional love and acceptance, Cole was touched by the tears rolling down Kelly's cheek. Oddly, Cole found no peace in the priest's words. The five hundred plus people seated in the cathedral were not the ones who needed to hear the message. There were a dozen or more street thugs, armed to the teeth, that terrorized, maimed, and killed innocent people who needed to be force-fed the words of the priest.

How different this service was from Ellie's. The muted light of the cathedral and the heavy robes of the priest gave the whole affair a gloomy, almost morbid, feel. Ellie's service was all sunlight and color. The hundreds of daisies that covered the casket were just an extension of the way she lived her life. The message that old Reverend Bates delivered was all about eternity. He spoke of the joys of heaven and how Ellie was free of the terrible disease that ravaged her body. He made heaven feel as if it was a breath away. The sunshine and daisies that filled the cemetery and service tent were like an invitation to one and all to answer his question, "Do you want to have eternal life and the knowledge of heaven like Ellie did?" with a resounding Yes!

Even the music was joyful. There were no dirges or sad melodies, no pipe organ. Ellie was sent away with *All is Well with My Soul* and *Amazing Grace*. For a moment Cole was awash in the pain of her death. He'd come so far, since they were reunited. The short time they were together had reignited their undying love and had healed years of pain, remorse, and regret.

But, today he was a new man, reborn in a way. His health, career and now, even Kelly, who, though not a replacement for Ellie, had become a source of goodness, optimism, and light just as she was. Cole was given a wonderful daughter, Erin. Although meeting for the first time as an adult, she is still as close and dear to him as if he had known her from birth. His granddaughter, Jennie, is such a delight. In her, Cole sees what Erin must have been like as a child. Erin and Jennie are loved and protected by a husband and father that every father wishes for their daughter. Cole Sage was a blessed man, and he was thankful. In the quiet of the massive cathedral, Cole closed his eyes and thanked the Creator for his many blessings.

The service ended with Holy Communion. Cole was the only one on his row who didn't go to the front of the church. As the pallbearers one by one returned to their seats, Cole received a combination of dirty looks and quizzical stares. *My 'protestant' must be showing* Cole thought.

As the casket rolled back up the aisle, Cole smiled at Kelly and she touched his arm as he passed. There was to be no graveside service. Chris' wishes for his funeral service had been clearly outlined in the papers he kept in Chuck's top dresser drawer. Until Chris' death, Chuck was never interested in looking in the hand-carved, teak box from Malaysia. It turned out that it held several important documents; Chris's will, social security card, birth certificate, and three letters to Chuck written over their fifteen years together. Chuck told Cole that the day after the shooting he had burned the letters without reading them. "There is only so much space for grief, and I'm full up," he said.

The final item on Chris's funeral plan was a party at Bimbo's 365 Club. Had Cole been by himself, he would have walked the half mile to the nightclub on Columbus, but it seemed a long trek for Kelly in heels, so he hailed a cab. The truth is, had he been by himself, he wouldn't have gone at all. They decided not to fight the parking chaos and left Kelly's car at the church.

"We don't have to stay, do we?" Cole asked Kelly, as the cab pulled to a stop in front of Bimbo's 365.

"Not if you don't want to," Kelly reached over and squeezed Cole's hand.

"Driver, can you go once around a couple of long blocks?"

"Yes sir!"

The cab pulled away from the curb and accelerated down Columbus. Cole and Kelly sat silently as they moved through the mid-morning traffic. Cole looked out the window and tried to figure out a way to not make an appearance at the wake. What he really wanted to do was go back to his office and start making calls. There needed to be answers and accountability for the senseless bloodshed at the parade. Chuck Waddell wouldn't be back to the office for a couple of weeks. The assistant editor would be filling in and would be doing good just to keep the presses rolling. Cole decided that his next story would be getting to the bottom the Chinatown Parade Shootings.

As they approached the corner of Powell and Filbert, a small yellow box school bus pulled up alongside the cab at the stop sign. Cole looked up from the cab into the round face of a Hispanic boy who showed the distinctive features of Downs Syndrome. As their eyes met, the boy gave Cole a huge grin. Cole gave the boy a big smile and waved.

The boy turned in his seat and made big circular windmills in the window. He mouthed something excitedly, but Cole couldn't make out what he was trying to say.

"What are you doing?" Kelly said with a giggle.

"I was waving to the kid in the bus. He's going crazy waving and laughing." Cole rolled down the window. "What?" he said cupping his hand behind his ear.

The boy slowly and clearly said, "I love you!" As he spoke he pointed at himself, made a heart with his thumbs and index fingers, and then with an exaggerated motion pointed at Cole and laughed happily.

"I love you, too!" Cole shouted out the cab window.

Kelly leaned across Cole to try and look up and out of the window, but the bus began to roll. The cab turned north up Columbus and the bus turned south on Powell.

"See, there is still fun in the world if you grab it as it comes!" Cole took a deep breath and rolled up the window.

"Marco! Sit down!" the bus driver yelled. The Hispanic boy was still waving out the window, though the cab disappeared from sight.

The boy plopped down hard on the seat. "He said he love me too! Mei, he said he love me! You hear him?"

Across the aisle a small Chinese girl, in heavy horn-rimmed glasses, sat giving Marco a quizzical look. "The window is closed. Nobody can hear him, silly."

"He said it. He said it," Marco repeated.

"OK," Mei Chou said softly, "You could hear it."

"OK, he said it. Love is good," Marco gave Mei an enormous smile. "I love you, Mei!"

"Oh stop it Marco!" Mei threw her hands over her face and rocked back and forth in the seat.

The other kids on the bus paid little attention to the two gigglers. The students of Golden Gate Training Center varied widely in the severity of their mental and physical development. In the case of Marco and Mei, they were among the higher functioning kids with symptoms of Downs Syndrome. The center was helping them learn life skills, as well as modified academics, to make them capable of independent living. They were old friends who had been at the Center since junior high. Now, as part of the senior class, they were being weaned more and more from the guidance and constant supervision they had received for so many years.

This year they were given responsibilities and jobs in and around the school to give them the confidence and experience they would need to find and keep a job. Marco worked in his family's Mexican restaurant evenings and on weekends. Mei, on the other hand, had been sheltered and smothered by her parents since birth. Her parents were successful merchants and ran an import business in Chinatown. She struggled with the thought of independence. Her parents, though supportive, were hesitant to embrace the idea of her striking out in the world on her own, no matter how limited. Mei was the baby of the family and six years younger than her closest sibling and almost fifteen years younger than the oldest. They intended for her to stay under their wing until they died.

The thought of what would happen then never entered their minds.

"Everybody out! The Disneyland Express has reached *Trainingland*!" The bus driver used his microphone to send the occupants of his bus into squeals of delight and scattered yells of "Oh Sal!"

The Golden Gate Training Center was a former parochial school which the archdiocese of San Francisco sold to the non-profit for a dollar. The pillared entrance and big, green door were intended to welcome the students with a nonthreatening feel. The halls and classrooms were far from the typical industrial greens and beiges of most "training centers". Instead each area of the school was decorated in yellows, soft pastels, and grassy greens. Even on the foggiest San Francisco mornings, the décor was like walking into springtime.

The staff was a jovial mix of longtime Special Ed teachers, social workers, and fresh, young college grads with degrees in Alternative Education and Psychology. The "mother superior" of the Center was a veteran teacher, educator, and administrator named, Maggie Strout. She may be just a few months from retirement, but she showed no signs of slacking off. Confined to a wheelchair since a childhood bout with polio, Mrs. Strout was a fierce advocate for the rights of the disabled. The few times someone was foolish enough to see her chair as a sign of weakness, they found themselves on the losing end of the argument. Maggie Strout possessed an almost encyclopedic knowledge of the rights and laws regarding any group unable to advocate for themselves due to mental or physical limitations. Both staff and students adored her.

This is not to say The Golden Gate Training Center was the Garden of Eden. Like any organization, there are those who don't fit the mold and rub and chafe just little enough not to be removed. Overall though, the workings of the school were such that both students and families loved the staff and facility.

Today though, Marco and Mei would see firsthand the kind of prejudice, hostility and cruelty the world holds for them. What they weren't prepared for, however, is what would be visiting their favorite class.

THREE

"Thank you, Chief Fitzgerald. Good morning, ladies and gentlemen. The Mayor will now make a few remarks regarding the recent tragedy at the Chinatown New Year's Parade. We will then a have a brief opportunity for questions. Mr. Mayor." Sandra Clements, the press officer for the Mayor's office, yielded the podium.

"Good morning, ladies and gentlemen. I think Chief Fitzgerald has summed up the facts of this case very well. Thank you, Chief. What I want to talk about is what these senseless shootings mean to the people and City of San Francisco.

As a boy my mother had a favorite song. She must have sung it a million times. 'If you're going to San Francisco be sure to wear some flowers in your hair'.

As we approach the spring and summer months this City comes alive. There is a special magic to the history and atmosphere of our city that draws people from around the globe who want to experience that special something that we all love. In 1967 San Francisco became famous for the "Summer of Love". I will not allow this summer to be known as the "Summer of Blood".

I would call on all of our citizens, Black, White, Chinese, and Hispanic to look into their hearts, into their neighborhoods and communities, and ask themselves, "Is this the kind of city we want?" A place where our citizens are not safe attending one of our oldest and best loved traditions, The Chinese New Year's Parade? I'm asking you please, if you know of anything that will help bring the perpetrators of this senseless and despicable crime to justice, call the hotline that should be at the bottom of your television screen.

As a people, and, as the community of peoples within San Francisco, we cannot and will not become captive to lawless thugs who care neither for our city nor for our traditions. You have my word, as Mayor of this amazing city, that I will, along with Chief Fitzgerald and the men and women of the best police force in the world, bring an end to this violence and bring back the comfort, safety, and magic to our streets once more."

Cole turned and walked away from the television in the lobby. On the elevator ride to his office, Cole slipped off his tie, rolled it, and shoved it down in his jacket pocket. His reflection in the shiny, brass elevator walls looked oddly strange to him. The dark suit was far from his normal work wear. Cole put his thumbs in his ears, wiggled his fingers, and stuck out his tongue at his reflection. He grinned at his own foolishness. As the doors opened he felt completely satisfied with himself.

"Good afternoon, Mr. Sage. Messages. There is a young man waiting for you in your office." The gray-haired, un-smiling secretary from the clerical pool thrust her hand out with several pink message slips.

She irritated Cole. Virgie was a grump. She didn't like him and it was very evident from her sneers, tone, and curt notes she frequently left on his desk. Maria, a cheerful little cutie with big eyes, and a "guess what I've been up to" smile, worked as Cole's secretary since he came to the paper. She went out on maternity leave and decided not to come back. Since then, the position was put on rotation with the sub pool. Virgie, with her girth and grimace, had occupied the desk for the last two weeks. "Occupied" be-ing the key term, because it had been an occupation, and about nine days too long to suit Cole.

"Who is he?" Cole asked.

"Your new intern."

"My what?"

The woman shrugged and spun her chair around to answer the phone. "Cole Sage's office."

"Take a message."

Cole opened the door to his office. He stood for a long moment looking at a figure sitting in a side chair, obscured by the morning's paper.

"Good Morning?" Cole said his hand still on the door knob.

There was no response. "Good morning!" Cole said a bit louder, the tone of welcome gone from his greeting. Still the figure sat unmoved.

Cole crossed the short distance from the door to the motionless figure and grabbed the top off the newspaper and gave it a swift yank upward.

Smiling up at him was Anthony "Whisper" Perez. "Hi, Cole."

"Anthony! What are you doing here?"

"I'm your new intern!" Anthony said jumping to his feet.

Cole gave the handsome young man a bear hug. He hardly recognized the person standing in front of him. Gone was the flannel-shirted hoodlum he first met in the southern California Mexican bar. Instead, a clean shaven young man, in grey slacks and a camel blazer, with a fresh haircut, and a stiffly starched powder blue oxford cloth shirt, stood grinning at him.

"I can't believe it! How'd this all happen? Why didn't you tell me you were coming?"

"When the University said I needed an internship for my Masters, I called Mr. Waddle and asked him if it were possible to do it with you. He said he would take care of it. So, here I am." Anthony grinned. The hoarse whisper was not as pronounced as when they first met, but the damage of his throat being slit still was evident.

"You look terrific. I love the glasses," Cole said, like a proud father.

Anthony self-consciously pushed the round, wire-framed glasses up on the bridge of his nose.

The phone rang.

"I thought I said take a message," he called through the open door.

"It's the police!" The voice came through the door with a harsh blast of sarcasm.

Cole smiled at Anthony and did an exaggerated raising of his eyebrows as he picked up phone.

"Cole Sage."

"Hey Cole, Leonard."

Leonard Chin was one of San Francisco's best detectives. Cole and Chin not only had a strong working relationship but they were just something short of being friends. Not to say that Leonard Chin wasn't great for a quick lunch meeting in some hole in the wall Korean or Chinese culinary wonderland, just don't expect an invitation to his house for dinner. He gave Cole some good solid leads for stories from time to time, and in return Cole was always willing to share information with him.

"We had another shooting last night," Chin continued, "looks like it's connected to the Parade mess. Two dead. You're on the Parade witness list so I grabbed you. Isn't Kelly Mitchell a friend of yours? I grabbed her too. I'm doing follow up." Leonard Chin was as matter of fact as a Detective could be.

Chin knew very well Kelly and Cole were more than "friends". It was just his strange way of trying to be funny.

"Yes, Kelly was with me. Where was the shooting?" Cole asked.

"16th and Potrero, Bunch of CPC Locos, across from McDonalds. They were hanging out in front of the brick warehouse there."

"Seems like a long way from Chinatown. Are you sure it was connected?"

"A woman leaving Safeway saw a car full of Asians blow through the light and open fire. Of course she has no idea what color, what kind, or how many of these guys were in the car."

"How'd she know they were Asian?" Cole asked.

"I quote, 'it had one of those pagoda thingies on the mirror'. You know, we all have those right?" Chin said sarcastically.

"Or a fat bellied Buddha on the dash," Cole quipped.

"So can we get together later? I'll take your statement," Chin said.

"That would be great, there's somebody I want you to meet."

"Tognetti's?"

"That would be great, three-ish?" Cole asked.

"Done. See you then."

Cole turned and smiled at Anthony. "Looks like it's time to go play journalist!" Cole quickly flipped through his messages and tossed them on the desk.

"That's why I'm here," Anthony said already standing by the door.

"Got a pen?" Cole asks rummaging around on the top of his desk.

"Here." Anthony tossed Cole a pen.

"Thanks," Cole said making his way to the door." Now what are you going to write with?"

"Oh, OK I see how this is going to be!" Anthony laughed, and followed Cole out the door.

The Tamale Parlor sits between an awning manufacturer and a linen supply company and has the reputation of having the best tamales in the city, possibly the world. For four generations it's been owned by the Gutiérrez family. The dream has always been to pass down the restaurant to the next generation in the Familia Gutiérrez, but the only child of Tito and Josephina was born with Downs Syndrome.

Marco was a happy baby and a delightful child, but as he nears his eighteenth birthday it is apparent, as high functioning as he is, he will never be able to take over the Tamale Parlor. That is not to say he doesn't do a wonderful job greeting people, serving their drinks, and occasionally taking their order, but the pressure of much beyond that has shown Marco's limitations.

The happy smiling boy that greets customers at the door with, "Welcome to the Tamale Parlor, Let me show you to your seat!" is loved by the regulars and, even though a surprise to new customers, Marco quickly wins them over.

The customers of the Tamale Parlor are a mix of neighborhood blue collar workers from the surrounding industrial businesses and suits in high-end luxury cars. It's a somewhat noisy atmosphere, where lunch time relaxation meets unobserved business meetings. Million dollar deals have been made over a plate of cheese and jalapeño tamales.

There is one job that Marco is never allowed to do in the restaurant. Even on the busiest day, Marco does not clear tables. Luis made the decision when Marco was about ten that having his son bus tables would look as though, "he was retarded and that was all he could do". He may have some handicaps, but he was still Luis's only son and he would have a position of dignity in his place of business.

Marco was also in charge of playing music from the jukebox. Luis taught him where the "free play" switch was when he was eight. The selections were an odd mix of Canciones de Mexico and Doo Wop oldies. Marco's favorite was Oogum Boogum by Brenton Wood, but the rule was no more than three plays in an afternoon shift. Marco knew his mother's favorite song was Carazon Viajero by Tish Hinojosa. When things got quiet after the lunch rush, Marco would go over to the jukebox and push D13. It was always followed by a "Gracias mi querido hijo" from the kitchen.

When two men in expensive suits came through the

door, Marco gave them his standard greeting. One man smiled warmly and called Marco my name.

"Your usual seat, Eric?" Marco asked.

"You betcha, buddy. I brought my friend for one of your mom's green chili tamale specials."

"And to drink sir?" Marco put on his best high class waiter voice.

"Diet Coke. Gil?"

"Just water for me," Gil said cheerfully.

"Right this way, gentlemen," Marco said leading the way to the table next to the jukebox.

Most of the lunch crowd was gone and a peaceful calm had come over the restaurant. Josephina came out from the kitchen and greeted the two men.

"Your regular?" she asked.

"Yes, Senora. For two." Eric replied.

The two men settled into their seats, Marco brought chips and salsa and went for their drinks.

"Nice little place," Gil said looking around.

"My dad used to bring me here when I was a kid. He worked just up the street."

"Cool place to celebrate!' Gil did a soft drum roll on the top of the table. "I think we just may have made the best deal in San Francisco history!"

"Or at least since the Gold Rush."

Marco came with the drinks.

"Nice kid," Gil said as Marco left the table.

"I've watched him grow up. "Sucks he's..." Eric paused, "...you know. He's the only kid and this place has been in the family for almost a hundred years."

The mood chilled a bit as Gil looked around the restaurant.

"So, escrows closed and we own an office building. Now what?"

The last customer paid their check at the counter and the busboy cleared their table. The jukebox was serviced earlier and this was the first chance Marco had to look at the new selections.

"415 McClarren. Got quite a ring to it," Eric offered.

"Hey, Marco what do you think?"

"About what?"

"415 McClarren. How's it sound?"

"Like a fast car?" Marco replied, a bit confused about why he was being asked.

"It's our new office building!" Eric said like a little kid with a new bike.

"OK," Marco said, and went back to reading the new titles.

"I think we should have a real classy brass sign splashed across the wall next to the front doors. My worry though is how long it will take to renovate. The three bids from the architects all said at least six months," Gil said, taking a scoop of salsa with a tortilla chip.

"I bet if we push we can get it done in three," Eric reassured.

"Problem is, none of them could start for at least six weeks."

"Until then," Eric stopped, as Tito approached the table with two steaming plates.

"Anything else gentlemen?" Tito asked.

"This is beautiful!" Gil said, smiling up at Luis.

"We're good. Thanks Tito."

Eric took a big forkful of tamale and raised it in a mock toast, "To 415 McClarren!"

"415 McClarren," Gil said, touching a matching forkful to Eric's.

"Did they give you a key? I didn't even notice."

"I'll call to get it re-keyed when the work starts. If you
need to get in, there is a key next to the 'Service Entrance'
sign at the back door. It's in an electrical box. The backdoor key is in there."

Eric put the forkful of tamale in his mouth as Brenton
Wood's Oogum Boogum falsetto added to the celebration.

Marco walked away from the jukebox and put one
hand up on an imaginary steering wheel and used the other to run through first and second gear on his imaginary
shifter, "415 McClarren race car, 415 McClarren fast car,
415 McClarren Marco's car, 415, 415, 415 McClarren,"
Marco chanted as he raced his way to the kitchen and out
of sight.

Marco's mother beamed at her son as he came through
the swinging door into the kitchen. "How was school today, hijo?"

"Good and bad."

"Bad? You never say bad. What happened?"

"First good, mama, first good." Marco smiled. "A man
in a taxi smiled at me. I was in the bus. I said, 'I love you'
to him. He yelled 'I love you too' to me! That was good."

"Love is good, hijo. But, I don't know if you should tell
men in taxis."

"Love everybody!" Marco said, showing signs of getting frustrated.

"Ok, Ok, So tell about the bad. What happened?"

"Miss Parra is mean. She yelled at Mei."

"Who is Miss Parra? I don't know that name." Josephina tried not to show her concern.

"She's new. I don't like Miss Parra. She's mean." Marco began to rock gently, a sure sign he was upset. "She called Mei mean names."

"Why would she call names, hijo?" Josephina said gently.

"Mei showed her, her, her drawing and she and she..." Marco's rocking quickened.

"Shh, shh, slow down. It's Ok, I'm listening."

"She spilled water. Miss Parra yelled at her. She, she, she called her 'clumsy idiot'. That's mean talk."

"Yes it is, hijo. We don't say mean things."

"Miss Parra is mean. I don't like her."

"Ok, well maybe she was having a bad day." Josephina's words seemed hollow to her even as she spoke them.

"I wish I had a 415 McClarren. I'd go drive away with Mei. No mean words." Marco's words trailed of as he drifted into his own thoughts.

FOUR

Anthony sat quietly through the late lunch meeting with Leonard Chin. The Detective was a very stiff man with a wicked sense of black humor. It seemed there was nothing sacred when it came to one of his hilarious verbal slashes. Cole gave, bobbed, weaved, and returned as good as Chin gave out. To Anthony's amazement, neither man gave more than a slight grin at the other's remarks. It seemed that part of the game was not to show the other their amusement at their wit. Anthony laughed aloud twice at the beginning of the meeting, but the silence at the table after was deafening. From that point on he showed little or no response to the irreverent lunch banter.

The interview with Cole, however, took a very serious tone. No clever remarks, jokes, puns, or barbs. It was straight ahead police work, the kind that several years before was not unfamiliar to Anthony.

"How many shooters did you see?" Chin began.

"Three to four on each side I guess."

"Guess?"

"OK, Three to four shooters on each side."

"Could you identify any of the shooters if you saw them again?"

"The Asians, maybe; the Mexicans, definitely not. They mostly had their backs to me."

"Alright, tell me about the Asians."

"White t-shirts, jeans, and khakis. Lots of tats. White flat-brimmed baseball caps with FCBZ stitched in black and silver. Young, late teens, early twenties," Cole said trying to pull back mental images.

"Doin' good," Chin said as he wrote in his black leather note pad. "Any facial characteristics you remember?"

"I was so worried about Kelly, I didn't really try to focus on the shooters until the firing stopped." Cole looked over at Anthony. "I really tried to register tattoo designs, something, anything, that could help, but it was such chaos and they all ran so fast after the fact, I really have nothing."

"That's OK." Let's go back to before the shooting started.

"The Norteños..."

"How do you know they were Norteños?" Chin interrupted.

"They were all flamed up. Lots and lots of red."

"Alright, go on."

"The Norteños beat on a guy in the crowd. Not sure what that was about. He took some pretty good licks. Did he come forward?" Cole inquired.

"No. Let me do the questions for a while, Newsboy," Chin jibed.

Cole shrugged and winked at Anthony.

"So, what was the first you knew there was going to be trouble?"

"I was about a hundred feet from where I had been sitting. I saw the Asians come from the crowd. To my right there was suddenly lots of red coming off the curb, then the shots. Only a couple at first, and then pow, pow, pow! I have no idea how many, but it was like strands of firecrackers going off. Mostly small caliber, .22s maybe. Then the big stuff. Cannons, Glock tens? 9mm at the smallest. Maybe a .35 or a 45 even. Big booming shots."

"Then?"

"I rushed back to Kelly. I pulled her to the ground. I really tried to take in the scene, because I knew I would be interviewed. But, I have nothing concrete."

"Just a bit more. When you found Chris Ramos, what can you tell me?"

"The dragon had collapsed. I lifted it off where he was lying. I saw, I recognized his shoe. He was obviously dead," Cole's voice faded off.

"That ought to do it. Thanks, buddy," Chin said.

"Pretty weak."

"I've gotten worse. Don't beat yourself up. Who the hell thinks they're going to be a war correspondent at a parade?"

The three parted company with Cole assigning his young protégé with the task of gathering background and color for the series they would work on about the Parade Shootout. Leonard, wished them well and promised to follow up with any information, in other words, an exclusive angle on the story. Cole picked up the tab.

Anthony didn't want to admit it, but he really wasn't

sure how he was going to start. Writing articles for the University of Chicago Maroon was on home turf. College kids are usually approachable for an interview. Once you get them started, you have a hard time getting them to shut up. This was different. Cole said to gather background. That required talking to people. In this case, people in Chinatown. Anthony knew from his own life, that communities like the one he grew up in, were tight, protective, and closed mouthed to strangers.

Look casual, Anthony thought. He stood for a long moment outside Starbuck's staring at the Chinatown Gate. A sip of his coffee, a deep breath, the orange hand changed to the green walking man, and ready or not, Anthony Perez was walking into Chinatown a reporter.

"Here we go," Anthony said, crossing Bush Street.

The green tile, arched entry to Chinatown was crowded with tourists. Buses full of European, Australian, and Japanese tourists were let off down the street. Two abreast and single file they followed tour guides waving little colored flags onto Grant Street and the exotic wonders to come.

For nearly half an ,hour Anthony walked up and down Grant, looking at the vast array of merchandise cluttering the sidewalk in front of the shops. He studied menus on restaurant windows and wandered down the occasional side street. To his embarrassment, he hadn't spoken to a soul.

A badly bowed and very old Chinese man was standing in front of his vegetable stall giving orders to a young woman as Anthony approached them. The old man slipped just inside the door as Anthony greeted the young woman.

"Good afternoon."

"Hello."

"I'm from the Chronicle can I ask you a couple of questions?"

"I guess so," the young woman said, not looking up from her work.

"I suppose you heard about the tragic shootings at the Parade," Anthony began.

"No."

"The shootings at the Chinese New Year's Parade?" he said in disbelief.

"No." The young woman continued to straighten the vegetables.

"Do you think there has been an increase in gang activity in Chinatown in recent months?"

"No."

The old man began moving toward Anthony and his employee.

"Are there any Chinese people in San Francisco?"

"No."

"Thought not," Anthony replied.

"You buy vegabull?" the old man demanded.

"I was looking for real Chinese vegetables. The young lady said there were no Chinese in San Francisco, so I guess I have to wait until I get to LA."

The young woman giggled softly.

"No talk. No buy. Go away." The old man took a broom leaning against the wall and began sweeping toward Anthony.

The old man said something in Chinese to the young woman and she scurried inside the shop. Anthony was emboldened by his first encounter with the residents of Chinatown and spent the next hour going up and down the street attempting to get something, anything out of the merchants, clerks, and anyone else standing still.

"This is just like home," Anthony said as he was briskly asked by a waiter to leave the Eastern Gate Restaurant.

The tall man in the crisp white shirt and black pants all but physically put Anthony out the door.

"Not a Chronicle subscriber, huh?" Anthony quipped as the waiter continued to scold him in Chinese. "All I wanted was a bowl of noodles."

Anthony shrugged and walked on. Out of the corner of his eye he saw a teenage girl looking at him.

"Hi," Anthony said moving towards her. "I'm from the Chronicle, can I ask you a couple of questions?"

"I know who you are. Someone wants to talk to you," The girl offered.

"That's one in a row."

Without any reaction, the girl turned and walked back toward Pine Street. As they approached the stoplight at an intersection, the girl didn't slow or break stride and walked right through the traffic. Anthony paused at the curb, saw a break in the line of cars, and darted across the street. About thirty yards later the girl ducked into an alcove between two shops. There was nothing but a steel grated door and a door bell.

"Where are we going?" Anthony asked.

There was no reply. The girl pushed the stained ivory button and the door buzzed and made a metallic click. She pushed the door open, crossed the small entry, and began to ascend a steep flight of stairs. Anthony looked at the bare wall to his left and the small collection of brass mail box doors on his right.

This is what you came for, he thought, and started up the stairs. At the top of the stairs the girl waited in a hallway lit only by a frosted window at the far end. About halfway down the hall she knocked on a door. As the door opened, she turned, and looked Anthony in the eyes for the first time. She gave him a sneer, blew out of her nose, and went back toward the stairs.

Standing in the doorway was a young Chinese man in his late teens or early twenties. He was about the same height as Anthony but much thinner. His crisp white, oversized t-shirt hung like a drape on his thin shoulders. On the bill of the white baseball cap he wore was a gold size and label sticker, across the crown was emblazed FCBZ in black and silver thread.

A rush of excitement shot through Anthony. This is the source. This is more than background. I can really get a story. His mind raced trying to formulate his first question.

"You the newspaper guy?"

"Anthony Perez, I'm with The Chronicle."

The thin young man stepped to the right side of the doorway and motioned Anthony in. In a moment, Anthony's excitement turned to apprehension. As he took in the room, he counted six young Asians in FCBZ ball caps. This was no simple interview. These guys had a message to deliver.

The obvious top dog sat a round table at the far end of the room. The surface of the table was cluttered with ashtrays, beer bottles, and several tattoo magazines. The man at the table sat with his back to the window and formed a dark silhouette against the bright incoming light.

"Have a seat." The seated man instructed.

Anthony crossed the room and pulled out a chair across from the seated man.

"Why you bother the people in my neighborhood?"

"I didn't mean to. I was just trying to gather some information," Anthony's tone was firm and matter of fact.

"They don't like it. That means we don't like it. That means I really don't like it."

"I get that. You don't like it."

The man flipped the lid on a dark, burgundy colored box on the table and took out a small cigar. Anthony wasn't so far removed from the street that he didn't recognize a "blunt", a hollowed out cigar filled with marijuana. The idea being that you could smoke it in public without anybody knowing what it was. From the smell of the very first cloud of smoke that crossed the table, Anthony could tell the Firecracker Boyz held some pretty strong cannabis.

"I'm Johnny Zhuó. My crew calls me Trick. You can call me Mr. Zhuó." He took a deep hit on the blunt.

"Alright. So how would you like to do an interview for the paper?"

"Mr. Zhuó." He looked around for approval from the others in the room. They obliged by giving a soft chuckle.

"Mr. Zhuó," Anthony added.

"What you want to know?"

"I would like to record our conversation so I don't forget anything or make a mistake." Anthony pulled a small digital recorder from his pocket, paused and said,"Mr. Zhuó."

"You want some of this? Good shit."

"I'm good," Anthony said declining the offer to share Zhuó's blunt.

As Anthony laid the recorder on the table between them, Zhuó's eyes narrowed. He slowly blew out a very fine plume of smoke. In what seemed a frozen lapse of time, Anthony realized Zhuó was staring at the faded XIV tattooed between his thumb and index finger. Although Anthony was going through the laser treatments to remove it, the faded blue ink was still clear enough for any-one acquainted with the gang identification.

"OK, first question. Who controls Chinatown?" Anthony hoped this obvious bow to the assumed power of the FCBZ street gang would not betray his increased heart rate.

Zhuó gave an exaggerated laugh. The rest of the room exploded in a show of gang pride and bravado.

"What part?" Zhuó said stilling the room.

"Let's start with that blend you're smoking." Anthony smiled, trying to look confident.

"They call it *Big Buddha Cheese*," the room once again burst into stoned laughter. "For sure not for Norteños." Zhuó gave Anthony a cobra like stare.

"So let's talk about the Parade."

"Let's not."

"Why's that? You don't want to or you don't have any information worth sharing?"

Zhuó took another deep hit. He was beginning to show signs of the effects of the powerful strain of weed. His lids were drooping just a bit. His gaze was unblinking, though, as he repeatedly drew a small circle on the top of the table. Anthony sensed the game was about to change but was unable to decide what to do.

"I was thinking it would be good to talk to someone at a newspaper. I wanted the people to know we are a com-munity minded group of Chinese-American young peo-ple. What I find is a Beaner snitch sitting at my table of hospitality."

Anthony laid both hands flat on the table top and leaned forward. "My name is Anthony Perez. I am a stu-dent at the University Of Chicago School Of Journalism.

I am currently working as an intern at the San Francisco Chronicle, while completing my Master's Degree. I resent being called a Beaner. I answer to no one except God and Cole Sage and he is available to verify what I'm telling you at The Chronicle." Anthony stared unblinking at Zhuó.

"What? You trying to be funny?"

"Why? Was it?" Anthony remembered Cole using that line on his friend Luis in LA once. He figured it might lighten the mood. It didn't work.

"Oh, I see, this is College Boy being a bad ass," Zhuó said contemptuously.

"I get it. I'm Mexican, therefore the other side. Frankly, I don't care what you thugs do. I'm just here to see if you had anything to say." Anthony stood up, picked the recorder off the table and turned toward the door.

Marco's favorite day at school was Art Day. He loved the feel of the tempera paint under his fingers sliding across the paper. The smooth wet colors swirl like a pretty melody from the jukebox at the restaurant. There are days he gets so lost in the gliding motion he forgets everything and everyone, but not today. It was not that kind of day.

"Miss Parra is really mean today," Marco whispered to Mei.

"I know, she's not nice to nobody."

The new aid was sitting in the corner with a don't-mess-with-me scowl. She growled, sneered, and scolded the kids in the class, until the door would open and a teacher or Administrator walked in. Then her countenance would change, and it was "honey", "sweetie", and a smile a yard wide.

Her mood swings kept the kids off balance and upset. Marco did his best not to look at her.

"She called Caleb a 'tard. She said it soft, but I heard," Marco whispered.

"You should tell on her," Mei returned.

"No way! I don't want my ear twisted again.

"Be quiet!" Came a harsh command from the aid.

Mei sat quietly not painting, not talking, not breathing. She was terrified of the new aid. Mrs. Stroud, their teacher, was getting ready to retire and was training a new teacher. She spent a lot of time in the room next door with the new teacher, leaving the aid alone in the room.

A boy named Adam, across the room, flicked blue watercolor with his paint brush and it hit the girl next to him.

"Don't!"

The squeal from the girl with the new blue freckles sent the room into an uproar. The aid crossed the room with angry strides. Adam, with the wayward paint brush, was laughing and pointing at the blue sprinkles on his neighbor's face and didn't see the aid's rapid approach.

"I am sick of your stupid antics!" Parra grabbed Adam's ear. "Get over here!" She hardly gave him a chance to get out of his chair before she began dragging the boy across the room.

As the aid and howling boy crossed the crowded room, Adam slammed into Mei's easel sending her cups of blue, red, and green tempera paint into a rainbow arch skyward. At the rainbow's end was the beige linen of Parra's pant leg.

"You little moron!" Parra screamed at Mei and, in a heartbeat, shoved her so hard she toppled over the easel and the empty chair next to her. "Look at my pants, you freak! You'll pay for this!"

"Stop it!" Marco shouted at the aid. He jumped to his feet and faced Parra. "Leave her alone."

"Stay away from me, you freak!"

Mei felt around on the floor for her glasses. Without them she was nearly blind. Even with the thick lenses, her eyesight was minimal. Her hands were wet with paint, but after a moment, she felt her glasses in the mess.

Marco pressed both his fists to his temples and closed his eyes tightly. "Leave her alone!"

Mei struggled to get to her feet. The floor was slick with spilled paint and water. Marco rocked back and forth where he stood, his eyes still tightly shut.

Parra kicked and shoved chairs, easels, and kids as she made her way to the door. As the door slammed behind her, the glass nearly shattered from the force. The hysteria of the class seemed to subside with the absence of Ms. Parra. Students came to the assistance of their classmates whose paint projects were turned topsy-turvy in the wake of Ms. Parra's rage.

Marco felt the gentle stroking of Mei's hand on his back. "It's ok. She's gone. It's ok," She said gently.

"Are you ok, Mei?" Marco's rocking was slowing. His eyes were still shut but the grimace was gone.

"My leg hurts. She made my pants dirty. Can you clean my glasses? My shirt is wet."

Marco took the paint-smudged glasses and wiped them as best he could on the tail of his shirt. "I hate this place! It's no good no more."

"I know. It sucks," Mei said, taking her glasses.

"Mrs. Strout doesn't like us anymore."

"Yes she does," Mei said sharply.

"Then where is she? Gone! That's where!" Marco slowly opened his eyes. "Ms. Parra is mean and hates kids like us.

She don't love everybody like Mrs. Strout used to. Love is good. Ms. Parra doesn't got love."

"Kids! Kids! What has happened?"

Marco and Mei looked at the door. Mrs. Strout rolled her wheelchair into the room.

"See. There she is!" Mei squealed with delight.

"Too late," Marco said softly.

The kids in the room rushed to the safety and comfort of their beloved teacher. All except Marco, he stayed back trying to decide what he wanted to do.

"Maggie, what on earth happened in here?" Mrs. Cline, the Principal, stood at the door taking in the multicolored disaster area.

"I'm not quite sure. Can you help me get everybody over to the desks that aren't covered in paint? I'll try and see if somebody can explain what happened."

"Ms. Parra ran into the front office saying something about being attacked," Mrs. Cline offered. "She's in the bathroom. She's pretty upset."

Mei stepped closer to Maggie Strout. "She got mad at Adam. She pulled his ear."

"Then what happened, sweetheart?" Maggie's voice was calm and reassuring.

"He knocked over my paints. It got on her. She got really mad."

Marco approached Maggie Strout for the first time. He was angry and his face was red. He took short, rapid breaths through his nose.

"Marco?" Maggie said, trying to size up the situation.

"She pushed Mei down. She called me a freak. I hate her."

"Marco, we don't hate, remember?" Maggie replied.

"You don't. I do. She's bad."

"Mrs. Cline. I think we need a change of scenery. Can we all go to the music room? We could have "Listening Time".

"Great idea," The Principal answered.

"Marco, how 'bout you and I walk together?"

"You talk nice. She's not nice."

"Mei, you can go with Mrs. Cline, OK? She'll help you get cleaned up."

Mei looked at Marco. He smiled but she knew he didn't mean it.

Maggie moved slowly down the hall with Marco at her side. She spoke but he wasn't listening. Marco decided what he must do. He'll tell Mei to meet him at 415 Mc-Clarren, and she will like his plan.

FIVE

Cole returned to his office from an editorial meeting around 4:50. Virgie, the secretary from the sub-pool, was packing up for the day and barely acknowledged his return. A small stack of pink message slips was in the middle of his desk. None from Anthony.

"Has Anthony, the new intern called in?" Cole asked through the open door.

"Who?" Virgie demanded.

Cole moved to the doorway, "Anthony Perez, the young man who was in this morning, the new intern, I went to lunch with. Five ten,160 pounds, dark hair, Hispanic, blue oxford cloth button down shirt, jeans, camel color blazer? Ring any bells?" Cole could hardly contain is disgust at this do-nothing inhabiting the secretary desk.

"Haven't seen him."

"Hasn't called?"

"Your messages are on your desk," The secretary said, without even looking in his general direction.

Cole watched as she opened the deep side drawer of her desk, took out her purse, picked up a *People* Magazine and an *I Love Kitties* coffee cup, and moved around the desk without closing the drawer, and started for the elevator.

"I won't be back."

"There is a God!" Cole said brightly.

"Asshole!" Virgie said, still walking.

"Charmer!" Cole said loudly at her back.

There was no response. Cole chuckled. He stood in front of his desk and he bent to see the numbers as he punched in Anthony's cell phone number. Five rings, then voicemail.

Cole reviewed his notes of the Chinatown shootings. He brought up the file with a rough outline and added a few thoughts. For a few minutes he worked on the introduction to what he hoped would be a piece to both honor those killed and injured, as well as cast a strong light on the menace of street gangs and the inroads they are making into the very fiber of the city. He made a good start, and after a bit of editing and review, he glanced at this watch. 5:30.

He hit the redial and speaker almost at the same moment and waited for Anthony to pick up. Five rings, then voicemail a second time. Anthony was one of the new generation of "connected" twenty-somethings that lived by, through, and for their phones. Cole was becoming concerned. He checked his cell. Plenty of battery and it was turned on. After a couple of attempts, he changed the ring volume to 'loud'.

Unable to fully focus, Cole continued to write. Glancing at his watch almost in rhythm with hitting the space bar and enter key. At 6:00 Cole hit redial again. Five rings then voicemail. He decided to go home.

Maybe Anthony lost his phone, the battery was dead, lost his number, fell off a Cable Car. For heaven's sake, Cole thought, he's not a baby. He didn't know where Cole lived, though. His bag was still at the office. Something just wasn't right.

Across town, Marcos and Mei each returned home. Neither told their parents of the day's events. Planted firmly in their minds were the seeds of what they must do before morning.

Mei emptied her backpack and hid the contents far under her bed. In its place she rolled and placed six pair of clean panties and a black bra. She carefully rolled and placed six clean t-shirts on the next row. A pair of jeans and a pair of black leggings went next. When she was sure her parents were asleep, she quietly went to the kitchen and got all the juice boxes and granola bars from the cupboard.

The backpack zipper was hard to close. But with patience and determination, Mei was able to get it closed. She patted the side of the Bratz backpack and, in the silence of her room, said, "I'm a grown-up now".

North of Market street, Marco cleared tables, served water, gave menus to the regulars, and played favorites on the jukebox. It was business as usual at the Tamale Parlor.

Had anyone been listening, they would have heard Marco repeating almost like a chant, "415 McClarren, backdoor, electric box".

The dishwashers seldom paid any attention to Marco. Truth be told, they were a bit unnerved by the boy with the strange eyes and thick tongue. So, when Marco entered the kitchen after the restaurant closed, they mostly kept their backs to him. His parents were in the tiny office in the hallway off the dining room counting the day's receipts.

Marco stashed the contents of his backpack under the seat of booth nine. He quietly made his way; backpack in hand, into the walk-in cooler in the kitchen. He took two plastic bags of freshly steamed tamales, a large bundle of grapes, a plastic container of salsa, and a plastic bag of tortilla chips and carefully arranged them in his backpack.

As he gently rocked back and forth at the end of the front booth, Marco sang a familiar tune with new lyrics,

Gonna live forever at 415 McClarren,
Nobody be starin' at 415 McClarren,
Me and Mei not carin' at 415 McClarren,
Gonna live forever at 415 McClarren.

Cole greeted the morning with an anxious stomach full of butterflies. He shaved, showered, and checked his cell phone three times for missed calls. A call to The Chronicle found no one picking up the phone in his office. Just as well, he thought.

The cross-town traffic was lighter than usual and he made the trip to Grant Street in record time. Merchants in Chinatown were busy setting up, sweeping, and hosing down the sidewalks. Cole approached a series of merchants with a big smile and asked if any were interviewed by a young man from the Chronicle. When he did get any kind of reply, it was curt, and made it quite clear they were not interested in talking to anybody not interested in buying.

On his way back up the street toward his car, he stopped at a fruit stand half-way up the block. A girl in her late teens was carefully arranging fruit and placing price cards.

"Good morning!" Cole said brightly.

"Good morning," the girl said softly.

"Beautiful produce."

"Thank you."

"What's good?" Cole said picking up an odd shaped orange.

"Everything," The girl replied with a coy smile.

"You're a lot of help," Cole returned her smile. "I think I'll try some of these."

Cole handed the girl three of the odd shaped oranges.

"These are good. Kind of sour, but in a good way."

An old man with a badly bent back came around the far side of the shop and stood studying the girl.

"I think we're being watched," Cole said in a mock whisper.

"Always," The girl giggled. "My grandfather thinks everyone is out to either steal from him or send him to China."

"How long has he been here?" Cole asked, as they made their way to the register.

"He was born here!" Her giggle showed the girl loved her answer. "That will be a dollar."

"Here you go," Cole said handing her four quarters.

"Thank you."

"Say, did you happen to see a young man from The Chronicle around here yesterday?"

"Hispanic? Kind of cute? Kind of a hoarse voice?"

"That's the one." Cole smiled at the ray of hope.

"Grandfather chased him off with his broom. He was asking about the parade."

"What time was that?"

"About three, I guess. Seemed nice."

"Very. Funny thing is we haven't heard from him. He's new in town and I'm trying to figure out where he went."

"Sorry..."

"Fruit not stock itself!" The old man called from behind the girl.

"She's a wonderful clerk!" Cole said loudly to the old man.

"Thank you," the girl mouthed handing him his small bag of fruit.

Cole winked and took his oranges and left the shop. Back on the sidewalk Cole wasn't quite sure how to proceed. Three o'clock was only a couple hours after they finished lunch.

The street was starting to fill with tourists. A couple more merchants with the same, closed mouthed response to Cole's smile and questions had him ready to call it quits. Two obvious gangbangers had been eyeing Cole from across the street since he bought the oranges. After a fourth rejection to his questions, Cole turned to face the pair in the white tees and FCBZ caps.

They just stood, arms crossed and staring back at him.

Cole darted between a cab and a minivan, and stepped up on the sidewalk next to the young men.

"Fire Cracker Boyz, huh?" Cole offered.

The pair just stood trying to look tough. Which, Cole thought, is pretty hard to do when you're five eight and a hundred and twenty pounds.

"So, are you going to tell me what I'm doing that you find so interesting?"

"You need to leave our neighborhood."

Cole looked unblinking into the eyes of the badly pocked face of the one who spoke.

"Why's that?"

"Trick says so."

"That him?" Cole indicated the non-talker.

"Trick gives the orders in Chinatown. He says you need to go."

"And if I don't want to?" Cole said looking at one and then the other.

"Pain," The non-talker finally spoke as he lifted the front of his t-shirt exposing the handle and trigger of a pistol.

"Even you guys aren't dumb enough to shoot a newspaper man on the streets of Chinatown. I'm bettin' Trick wouldn't like it. So how about you cut the tough guy crap and you tell me what I came here to find out?"

"What would that be?"

"Where's Anthony Perez, The intern who I sent down here to get information about the Parade shootings?"

For the first time the pair looked at each other. Pockmarks took a couple of steps away and raised his cell phone to his ear. He said several short bursts of Chinese into the phone.

"You come with us," He said spinning around.

"You got a name?" Cole asked.

"Not for you."

"Want an orange?"

The pair turned and walked up the street. They never looked back. They knew that Cole wouldn't be far behind, and he wasn't.

The Kowloon Dim Sum Restaurant was down a side street off Grant. The day was beginning to warm up, but the windows were completely steamed up. The inside of the Kowloon was like a sauna. Steaming pots in the kitchen filled the tiny space with the smell of steamed buns and dumplings. The air was thick, moist, and unpleasant.

Pockmarks turned the large metal lock behind him as he closed the door. A group of six white t-shirted young Chinese men were sitting, eating at a table against the wall. The steam in the room seemed to have taken a bit of the starch out of their crisp white t-shirts.

"Sit!" the young man at the end of the table said.

"Trick?" Cole inquired.

"Mr. Zhuó," He said, not looking up. "Trick is for my friends."

Cole set his bag of oranges down on the table and took a seat on one of the chrome and plastic chairs. "Why don't you open the door? It's like a sauna in here."

"She won't let us," Zhuó said, taking a bite of the snow white bun. "Says steam is good for your skin."

A flat faced woman in a stained apron came from the kitchen with a platter of sesame seed covered balls. The young men in the room didn't wait for the platter to even hit the table before they snatched and grabbed the balls from the plate. Like little kids at a birthday party, the group of street hardened thugs displayed what was their chronological age. They were all in fact, still teenagers.

"They like dessert."

"So do I." Cole reached for one of the last three sesame balls from the platter, "It means the meals over and we can talk."

"You need to learn to relax. Confucius says,"

"Really? Confucius? You are going to give me a Confucius quote?" Cole laughed. "This is like an old Charlie

Chan movie. Look, the tough guy posturing is fine. I get it. You're tough. Your boys are tough. You have Anthony. I want him back. What do you want?" Cole pushed the plates out of his way, set the uneaten ball down, leaned forward, and glared eye to eye with Zhuó.

"Omar Haro," Zhuó said, as he stacked two plates atop the other.

"Who's that?"

"A beaner."

"And?"

"He shot my cousin at the parade thing."

"And you think you're going to trade Anthony for that guy? You didn't think this one out very well. What? You think the police are just going to let you trade Anthony for a Norteño and all is forgotten?" Cole was getting a much better idea of who he was dealing with. With all the gangster movie civility Zhuó tried to portray, he was a just another street punk. And not a very smart one at that.

"You work for the newspaper right? You know people? Then make the deal. One more dead Mexican is nothing to me. My cousin will be dead for a long time. I can't change that. But your boy, I can make him dead too. That I can do. So, you do what you need to, to make a trade happen."

"If I go to the police with this, they'll arrest the whole lot of you. You have no chance of this working." Cole tried to hide is amazement at the stupidity of the conversation.

"Then we kill your Beaner schoolboy. He will be shark shit before the sun goes down. There are lots of sharks just beyond the Golden Gate, did you know that?" Zhuó's eyes were cold and without fear. "Habeas Corpus. No body, no crime. Isn't that the law?"

Cole just sighed deeply, not about to get into a jail-house law argument. "I'll see what I can do."

"How long does it take someone to starve to death?"

"I'm not sure," Cole lied.

"I'm sure as hell not wasting food on a guy who's gonna be dead. So I tell you what. You have two days."

"I'm not sure..."

"Then I hope the sharks like Mexican food!" Zhuó interrupted. The room burst into laughter. Zhuó just smiled. "Good-bye, mister?"

"Sage," Cole said as he heard the metallic clank of the door unlocking behind him.

Zhuó reached for another dumpling but his eyes never rose above the bamboo basket. The other three at the table stood as a signal for Cole to leave. The shortest one took an orange from Cole's bag, then handed it to him.

Outside Cole took a deep breath and blew it out slowly. The breeze up the narrow street felt good on his moist skin. He dropped the bag between his feet and interlaced his hands behind his head. Cole took another deep breath and looked up at the sky. He knew what must be done. The question was, could he do it?

Marco and Mei didn't catch the bus. It wasn't unusual. The bus driver just rolled past their stops. The plan was to meet at 415 McClarren. Mei was waiting when Marco arrived. He had gotten confused and hopped the wrong Muni Bus.

"Hi Mei!" Marco shouted, as he began running toward her.

"Where have you been?" Mei's voice betrayed her worry.

"I got on the wrong bus. I'm not lost though. I'm here."

There was a steady stream of foot traffic on McClarren as people rushed to their offices. Lots of briefcases and Café Espressos. Two kids with backpacks were barely noticed in the sea of focused early morning suits and pencil skirts. No one saw Marco and Mei as they went down the alley next to 415.

Above a rollup door at the service entrance were three faded stick-on house numbers that told them they had found the right building. Marco stood looking at the roll up door.

"How do we get in?" Mei said softly.

"The key is in the electrical box," Marco said, as if he knew what it meant.

"What's that?" Mei frowned.

"A box where electrical is," Marco replied, as he looked from one side of the huge wall to the other.

The pair spotted two groups of flat grey panels at almost the same moment. One by one they popped open the covers. Two were sealed with wire twists and they left them alone. The last box of the first group held the key. Hanging on a screw, two keys waited, just like the man in the restaurant said.

"Here they are Mei! Here they are! I told you!"

Mei peered into the panel, took the keys, and closed the door. As Marco watched, she walked to the door just to the right of the roll up and tried the key.

"This one works," She said excitedly.

They opened the door and entered the building. Marco locked the door and they made their way across the dimly lit room.

"I can't see very good," Mei said.

"Go to the light. I think it is a door."

Marco was right. The thin ray of light that lay across the floor was from the crack of a door left slightly ajar. It opened into a hallway leading to the front of the building. Natural light from the windows on the ground floor lit their way.

"It's all ours!" Marco said with delight.

"It's not ours. We are borrowing it for a while."

"Forever!"

"Let's go upstairs. I like to see out better."

In the lobby, four sets of elevator doors faced the front windows. Outside, the shapes of the morning foot traffic flickered past, their shadows melding together on the soaped out windows and huge front door.

"Up. Up. Mei."

"I know, Marco," Mei said, giving Marco a push on his shoulder. "Up we go." She pushed the button with the embossed upward arrow.

The doors opened almost immediately. The pair stepped inside. For a long moment they stood staring at the two long rows of black buttons.

"What floor?"

"High up!" Marco said excitedly.

"Twelve?"

"No, thirteen!"

Mei stood looking at the buttons. Slowly she raised her hand and ran her fingers over the buttons. "Ten, eleven, twelve, fourteen." She turned and faced Marco. "There's no thirteen. Look."

"Ha! They forgot. Fourteen!" Marco reached past her and pushed the fourteen.

The elevator jerked ever so slightly and began moving. Moments later the doors opened and Mei and Marco stepped out into the reception area of their new home.

"I like this. This is just right," Marco said looking out the floor-to-ceiling windows.

Mei walked cautiously toward a door to the left of the room. She slowly pushed the door open and stood silently. After a long moment, she stepped into a large conference room. The space was carpeted and light sliced the floor from the almost closed blinds. She turned and closed the door behind her exiting the room.

"Too big"

Marco didn't respond, he just stood looking out the window. Mei looked around and made her way to another of the three doors. Growing in confidence, she opened the door to find a short hall and two restrooms. She nodded and closed the door.

"Bathrooms!"

"OK", Marco said, not turning around.

The third door opened onto a long hallway. All the doors were closed and the hallway was dark and uninviting. Mei opened the doors one by one. Most were small offices, some had desks, some still had phones sitting on the floor. In the middle of the hall on the right side was a "Women" bathroom and on the left, a "Men".

Mei stood staring at the sign with the blue "Men" sign. This was a chance to see what was inside. Her brother Ricky always locked the bathroom door at home. He would say he had business to do. Mei never understood why at home everybody used the same bathroom, but at school boys and girls each had their own bathrooms. This was her chance to find out why.

She looked down the hall toward the reception area and Marco. He won't know, she thought. The door was on a strong pneumatic closer. Mei pushed hard, the entry to the unknown lay just ahead. A sensor turned on the lights as she stepped inside. Four sinks and tall mirrors lined the right wall. To the left were three stalls and four oval porcelain sinks hanging on the wall. Why do they need more sinks? Mei approached the strange fixtures. She was standing trying to figure out why the sinks had flushing handles, when the door opened behind her.

"You should pee in the girl's room. This one says 'Men'!" Marcos said with an authoritative scowl.

"I wasn't! I was just checking out the rooms!" Mei said indignantly, as she marched passed Marco and out the door.

"So where are we going to sleep?" Marco asked, following her into the hall.

"There are lots of rooms here. I guess we can have any one we want. Some even have desks. Let's check out the rest of the doors."

At the end of the hall, to their delight the duo found the break room. Marcos found the light switch and they said almost in unison, "Yes!"

There were three tables and chairs, a refrigerator, a stove, microwave, and large sink. Marcos opened the refrigerator and took out a plastic container.

"Gross!" he squealed as he lifted the lid on someone's long-forgotten mold-solid lunch. "I brought some grapes and other stuff. I'll put them in here."

"We've got a whole house here. Bedrooms, bathrooms, and a kitchen." Mei smiled at Marco, "I think this is great!"

"I told you we can stay forever! We got everything."

"Maybe you're right." Mei looked around the room. She nodded her head several times before saying, "We are grownups now."

Marco took off his backpack. "I'm hungry. You want a tamale?"

SIX

The phone on Cole's desk had far more buttons and gadgets than he would ever use. *What ever happened to just plain old telephones?* he thought. Six buttons, five of which he never used, stared up at him. The little grey screen was dark and reflected the lights overhead. Dial it. Funny thing is there are no dials any more. The whole world was buttons and touch pads. With all the changes, with the speed mankind was flying into the world of social media, communication, and technology, basic animal instincts still rear their ugly heads.

As he rolled and tumbled the night before, Cole realized what he needed to do. It went against everything Anthony fought so hard to get away from. He was a college graduate. His future was solid, and secured. This mess was and wasn't Cole's fault. Either way, the guilt was palpable.

Anthony was no longer the street hustler he met almost five years ago.

Cole picked up the hand set. A little red rectangle lit up on line one. He stared at the number scrawled across his old note book. The name above the number flooded Cole's memory. He saw a spark of something special in "Whisper" Perez the first time they met. He was bright, well read, and possessed a natural curiosity. The thugs he surrounded himself with were another story. Luis Hernandez's name carried dark fears as well as gratitude in Cole's thoughts.

The violence that Luis was capable of, without concern or a thought of the consequences, made this call all the more difficult. Cole could clearly see in his mind's eye the box cutter and Luis slicing open a man's scalp. If he would slice open a man's head for Cole, what was he willing to do for his lifelong friend? Savage cruelty without hesitation, and only ten digits away. Cole would be asking for what he knew would unleash unspeakable retribution.

Cole sat the handset down and decided to use his cell instead. He hit the numbers in rapid succession not realizing he was holding his breath. On the third ring he heard Luis' flat deep "Hello".

"Luis. This is Cole Sage. You remember me?"

"The guy who paid for Whisper to go to school. Yeah, I remember you. I ain't seen him in four years." Luis did not sound pleased.

"There's a problem."

"You are a problem old man. You bring it with you. What you want this time?"

"It's Anthony. Whisper. He's in trouble."

"What, you can't make him do his homework?" Luis chuckled at his joke.

"I wish it were that simple. He's been taken by an Asian gang up here in San Francisco."

"What the hell's he doin' up there?" Luis sounded angry.

"He was working with me, doing an internship with the college. He was on assignment and got too deep into their business, I guess." Cole tried to explain.

"You guess? Don't you know what he was doin'? I thought you always knew everything!"

"Look, I didn't know who else to call. The cops have nothing..."

"Never do," Luis interrupted.

"He's been gone two days. I met the guys who took him. They want one of theirs released from jail. It's never going to happen. It's a gang thing. Brown on yellow. Norteños verses unaffiliated Asians."

"So now schoolboy needs his old street shit friends to save his ass, ay?" Luis was almost growling.

"No, I do," Cole replied.

"This your best number?"

"Yes."

"I'll call when I get there." The line went dead.

Cole just sat with the phone to his ear. What had he done? He knew the knot in his gut would not soon dissolve. He was part of the violence he so detested. A means to an end? It's easy to justify if it's somebody else doing the deed. Cole would still have blood on his hands.

Anthony awoke with the iron taste of blood in the back of his throat. A dull throbbing in his shoulder and knees confirmed that he had been shoved down a flight of stairs. The last thing he remembered, before being swallowed by the darkness, was a voice behind him saying, "Don't trip". His wrists burned where he was strapped to a chair. A pair of florescent bulbs arced and sputtered over a small greasy workbench across the room. Anthony blinked and shook his head, the haze of his unconsciousness refused to clear.

The room was a disheveled collection of boxes, old furniture, and shelving crowded with bric-a-brac and dragons. The sound of footsteps, muffled laughter, and the thump, thump, thump of a boom box came from overhead. Anthony was concerned but not afraid.

The recklessness of the FCBZ, and Trick in particular, was not the way business was conducted on the streets of East L.A.

Anthony momentarily blacked out again. As he tried to shake the swamp of black ink from his head, he attempted to take inventory of what he was sure of.

There were at least ten guys upstairs. They were younger than he first thought. Teenagers, high school age for the most part, and mostly, really stoned. All were clearly willing to kill him, and certainly, the innocent bystanders at the parade. Why hadn't the police caught up with these guys? They were certainly visible. By now Cole must realize something was wrong.

The number of footsteps overhead seemed to be growing. Behind and above him came the sound of a door opening and steps quickly coming down the stairs.

"Hey, what's your password?" Ricky Chou shouted.

"Anthony closed his eyes trying to focus on the words. "What?"

"The password, for your phone! What is it?' The voice was connected to a pair of hands that shook Anthony's shoulder violently.

"I, I, what, what do you want?" Anthony tried to process what the voice was saying through the pain in his shoulder.

"Let me say it slowly." Ricky moved within inches of Anthony. He could smell a heady mix of marijuana and tobacco. "Your phone password, dumb shit!" the almond eyes widened and spit flew into Anthony's face from the force of the scream.

"Chicago2013," Anthony said, knowing it was better to give it to the guy, rather than get beat up, or worse.

Ricky Chou stepped in closer, but white t-shirt was all Anthony saw in front of him. "Thank you, Taco Man!" he chirped brightly.

Anthony looked up to see the grinning face of one of the FCBZ punks that filled the room upstairs. This was a face he would remember.

The grin disappeared and Chou slapped Anthony on the side of the head and said, "Don't go away!" and with a stoned giggle at his clever remark, he ran back to the stairs.

"*Taco man*? That's the best you got?" Anthony said, half smiling, his head clearing and his mind starting to work. "Now go turn on the GPS, pendejo."

Anthony watched as the errand boy scampered back up the stairs.

The door slammed behind Ricky Chou, "Chicago2013".

"That was quick."

"You sent the right guy, Trick!" Chou blustered.

"We'll see. Listen up. I have an idea. Let's set fire to some Norteño ass." Trick Zhuó stood and walked to the window. "Who'd like to take a little ride to the Mission?"

The Mission District, is a small neighborhood that upwards of 200 active gang members call home. Norteño gangs control between the south section of 26th Street to 20th. The Mission is not a place where Asian gangs are welcome or safe. Further north is controlled by various groups of the Sureño family of street gangs. Neither group would tolerate an intrusion from an unconnected bunch of Asian bangers in souped up Japanese "rice burners". The combination of the way they look and the cars they drive, make the FCBZ stick out like an olive in a jar of cocktail onions.

Trick nodded, not the least bit surprised, when he received unanimous support.

"Mr. Sage?"

A small blonde woman in her fifties stood at the open door.

"Yeah?" Cole waved her in dryly.

"I'm, Hanna Day." the woman's blue eyes twinkled with a mischievousness far younger than her fifty plus years.

"I'm Cole Sage." Cole stood and offered his hand across the desk.

"You're a lot taller in person than you are in print."

"What?" Cole said, not quite sure he heard right.

"Nothing. Um, I'm from the clerical pool. I'm here to man, uh, woman, the secretary desk." Hanna started to panic, fearing her attempt at jest was not welcome.

"Have a seat, please. Have a seat." Cole realized the disaster his office was in as Hanna picked up a stack of folders from the chair and looked for a place to set them.

"You're number three or four, I don't know, maybe five, to be sent up here. Frankly, I have run out of patience with all of you, 'I'm only filling in', *People* reading-fingernail polishing...

"Look," Hanna interrupted. I want this job. I asked for this job. I need this job."

Cole sat for a long moment looking at the woman in front of him. Gone was the cute, perky, pixie who just greeted him a few seconds before. In her place was a woman of intense conviction. She wasn't pleading, she wasn't even asking, she was telling him the way it was going to be, and he liked it.

"You may regret it at times, but you won't be sorry. I make mistakes, but I will work my heart out for you. I've read all your stuff since you've been here, and a lot of what you have done over the years. I can do whatever you need me to. Research, proofread, type, make calls. Please, please Mr. Sage, don't just have me answer calls. You don't know it now, but you need me as much as I need to..."

"I get it," Cole said softly. "Look, I ..."

"Just one more thing," Hanna said, raising her hand like a school girl. "I won't leave. I don't want to be a writer, or an editor's secretary. I want to be like Jean Arthur or Rosalind Russell in the old movies where they always help their boss. I want to..."

"I think maybe we should call the clerical pool," Cole said firmly.

Hannah's heart sank.

"And have them take you off the sub list." Cole continued. "Anybody who uses Jean Arthur in their pitch to get a job needs to be at that desk!" Cole laughed, showing the first signs of his true nature.

Cole had no idea that he had just won the lottery. Hanna Marie Day, was a survivor. Orphaned at five, she had survived years in the Foster Care system. She was mentally, physically, and sexually abused until she turned seventeen.

That's when she left her last foster "father" with a cracked skull, a pair of ruptured testicles, and a front door hanging on one hinge.

That summer she went to the California Conservation Camp and fought forest fires. She got a job as a monitor at a burglar alarm company at night and went to community college in the daytime. Married at nineteen, widowed at twenty-one, Hanna never gave up her dream of an education. It would be five more years before she re-enrolled at the University of California at Irvine and earned her degree in English while working at an all-night video store. At thirty she remarried and was happy until her first child was born with a genetic heart defect and died five days later. Her husband went out and got drunk with his brother and stayed that way for five years. By then Hanna was gone.

After twenty years of being unappreciated and underpaid, she was sitting across the desk from the man who wrote *Women, Abuse and Recovery: From Darkness to a Bright New Beginning*. Hanna still had a ragged, yellow copy in a sheet protector. It changed her life. She saw a new beginning each day, no excuses, she was in control of her life. The scars had faded and the anger and fear of abuse had been cast into a sea of forgetfulness. She set out four years ago to get this job and now it was hers.

Hanna sat silent, dumb struck by Cole's response. She came prepared with a lot more reasons she should get the job. This went far better than expected. In the other room the phone rang for the third time.

"Are you going to get that?" Cole's voice brought Hanna out of her thoughts.

"Yes, sir, yes. I'll get that."

Finally, Cole thought, somebody who is just crazy enough to do this job right.

The phone on Cole's desk buzzed. "Yep."

"Mr. Ehcoff, upstairs."

"Sage."

"Sage, what's the deal with the Chinese?"

"There's a lot of them, and they make crappy stuff."

"Funny. We've gotten a bunch of calls from Chinatown saying our people are harassing the merchants. You know anything about this? The description sounded a lot like you. The other guy I don't know about."

Cole was keeping a lid on Anthony's abduction. It was wrong. He knew it, but it needed to play out. No cops, no bosses, these were street rules. So he lied.

"No, I've heard we all have a doppelganger. Maybe mine has come to town."

"I don't think I'm getting the straight dope here. I know how you work. I don't like it. God knows why, but Chuck Waddle thinks the sun shines out of your ass. I don't. As long as I'm filling in, I don't want any problems. I can't fire you, but by God, I would be happy to put you on indefinite leave. Got it?"

"Crystal."

"That is a mixed metaphor."

Cole knew it wasn't, he just sat silently.

"Good, we're clear?"

"I got it." He set the phone down.

"If it's OK, I'm going to run back down to clerical and get my things," Hanna said from the doorway.

"Fine."

Hanna could tell from the look that Cole gave her that the request must have sounded a bit odd. "They told me I would probably be right back."

"Why's that?"

"They said you were impossible. Did you really chase off the others?"

"I prefer to think it was mutual."

"I prefer to think you were saving the spot for me." Hanna smiled and looked down at the floor.

The raid into Norteño territory was going even smoother than Trick imagined in his smoke muddled brain. The ease of how their two cars cruised into the Mission without being spotted gave Trick a misguided feeling of invincibility.

The streets were empty. Few cars were parked along the streets. Traffic moved in both directions on Folsom, nothing threatening, or even warranting a second glance. That was all fine and good, but Trick needed to find some "red". There was light foot traffic around a couple of corner markets, and a group of kids played soccer in a school yard, but not a Norteño to be seen.

Finally, after crossing 24th Street, Trick signaled and turned west on 25th.

"This was a waste of time," Trick snarled. "Let's head back."

Another empty street. Trick slowed to a stop and Ricky Chou hopped out of the second car and approached Trick's window.

"What's up?"

"Waste of time," Trick replied. "Let's head for home."

"Ahright, s'cool." Ricky nodded, and returned to his car.

Trick began to slowly roll forward. A second later he hit the brakes. His arm shot out the window and he began pointing frantically.

Ricky ran back to Trick's car to see two guys in red caps, red t-shirts, saggy jeans, and red sneakers walking down Balmy Street. The block between 24th and 25th was like an alley. The walls and garages seemed to be a gallery of murals with brightly colored Hispanic themes. The pair had nowhere to go.

"You guys circle and come up the other way. Go, go, go!" Trick said in a hoarse, forced whisper. "Be cool, be quiet!"

Ricky passed Trick's car slowly and almost silently. Once passed Balmy, he fairly flew around the block. Stealth like, Ricky Chou's lowered, silver Civic with blackout windows, pulled into Balmy alley almost unheard. It was too late for the pair to escape as they shared a joint and admired the myriad of murals. They were trapped.

At the first glimpse of Ricky's Civic, Trick's black on black Acura turned onto Balmy unnoticed. Like two sleek cats, ever so slowly, moving in on a mouse, by the time their prey saw them, it was too late.

All eight occupants of the two cars were out in a heart-beat and surrounded the two Mexicans.

"Buenos Dias, dead men."

The pair said nothing. Ricky stepped forward and took the still smoldering joint from the hand of the shorter Norteño.

"You are making a big mistake."

"No, it seems you have." Trick smiled.

"Good shit," Ricky said still sucking the smoke ever deeper into his lungs.

"Yo' you're on our turf here. You can do what you want for now, but you can't even deal with the shit that's gonna come down. You feel me? You're dead."

"You're right. We are going to do what we want. What happens next won't matter to you. Ricky take this one." Trick pointed at the silent one.

As instructed, Ricky moved in fast. With deliberate moves, he snapped the long red bandana out of the back pocket of his prey.

The young man spun about and spewed a barrage of Spanish profanity into Ricky's face. Trick nodded to a heavy set passenger from Ricky's car. With one powerful swing to the knees from the baseball bat he had concealed behind his back, he dropped the Norteño to his knees.

The talker rushed at Trick. Another FCBZ sent a cracking blow to his jaw, dropping him at Trick's feet.

"Get him in the car!" Trick ordered, pointing to the young man rolling on the ground holding his knee.

Two of the Asians grabbed him by the arms and yanked him to his feet. Ricky took the long red bandana and tied it over the Mexican's eyes making a hard tight knot across the bridge of his nose. The remainder of the rag Ricky shoved deep into his mouth as he swore and gagged. Within seconds he was shoved into the back of Trick's car.

"He's all yours." One of the FCBZ said.

As he struggled to get to his feet, the spokesman was pummeled with kicks, punches, stomps, and bone crushing blows from the baseball bats. As Trick backed out onto 25th street, the last thing he saw in Balmy alley was the limp, red form of the unconscious Norteño receiving two last kicks to the head. Ricky and his crew were running for their car and headed for home.

As Trick sped down 25th toward Folsom he looked in the rear view mirror. "I hope you're comfortable. We have something very special planned for you."

The other passengers laughed wickedly. The two in the back elbowed their hostage hard in the sides.

"How easy was that man? We should have done this a long time ago!" Curtis Doo stomped his feet and put his arm out the passenger side window. "What a rush, damn, what a rush!"

Trick smiled but didn't say a word, he just ran his second red light heading for home.

SEVEN

As Hanna settled in, it was apparent to Cole there was a whole new breed of cat filling the secretary desk out front. She returned from clerical with a small box and a grocery bag. He watched as she methodically placed the contents of the drawers on the desk top. At one point Cole heard her mumble, "What is all this crap?" A steady crunch and thud of things hitting the trash can continued for several minutes. Finally, Hannah picked up the waste paper basket and disappeared behind the sea of cubicles outside of Cole's office

Cole tried to keep his mind occupied with reviews of drafts, notes, and the bits and pieces he started for the article on the Parade shootings. Deep into his thoughts, and no longer facing the door, he didn't notice the person standing in the door way.

A dark haired woman with her hands shoved deep into

the pockets of her waist length leather jacket cleared her throat in an attempt to draw Cole's attention. It didn't work.

"Excuse me."

"Oh, sorry," Cole said looking up from his notes.

The woman entered the office, arm out, and offered Cole a business card. She was medium height with a solid build, and a no-nonsense gait to her stride. Her nearly black hair was pushed behind one ear. The other side seemed intentionally swept forward, but not for style. As she offered her hand to Cole, he could see that the side of her face and neck had been burned or severely injured in some way. His gaze, ever so brief, was long enough for the woman to self-consciously smooth the hair on the scarred side of her face.

"My name is California Corwin, Mr. Sage. Can I have a moment of your time?" Her voice was strong and confident.

"Alright, what can I do for you?" Cole replied.

"A mutual acquaintance said you have a lot of experience keeping things quiet."

"Except my big mouth." Cole smiled and offered her a seat.

"I have a client," she paused realizing that Cole just looked at her card, "I have a client that has a serious problem but wants no police and no press."

"Frankly Ms. Corwin, I'm not sure what, if anything, I could do about that. What sort of problem are we talking about?" Cole looked back down at the card that read California Corwin, Personal Investigations. No address, just a phone number.

"Please call me 'Cal', Mr. Sage."

"OK, then I'm Cole. So what's this all about?"

"My client is a Chinese business man named Cheung Chou. A wealthy business man. He and his wife, like most Chinese, are very private people. Family problems stay in the family and at the very most a small community of friends and trusted associates."

"A hard wall to breach," Cole said, watching Cal adjust in her chair.

"Indeed. They have a daughter."

Here we go, Cole thought. What could I possibly do about a pregnant, drug addict, hooker, truck driver, stripper, lesbian, weight lifter, stand-up comedian? Cole's thoughts were interrupted with the only thing that wasn't going to be on his list.

"She has Down Syndrome. For old school Chinese this is a very difficult thing to deal with. But my client and his wife are pretty progressive in their thinking. They've tried to accept and deal with the realities of their daughter's condition. She is in a very fine school for kids with her kind of limitations."

"That sounds wonderful," Cole interjected.

"It is, and they've seen her really blossom. The problem is, she's disappeared."

Cole sat straight up and leaned forward in his chair. "Kidnapped? They need to call the police. This is not to be handled by someone like you! No slight intended, but time is of the essence. They can't let pride or whatever it is get in the way of a proper investigation." Cole couldn't believe what he was hearing.

"Hold on." Cal's whole demeanor changed in a heartbeat. "Nobody said anything about kidnapping. She's run away."

"OK, I'm lost. The kid ran off, they hired you to do what? Find her? I don't see where I fit in the mix."

"I knew this was stupid," Cal said standing. "I was told you were good at putting two and two together. I'm new at this kind of investigation and I've hit a brick wall. I'm, sorry I wasted your time." Cal turned for the door.

"Geez, are you touchy. I didn't say I wouldn't help you, I just don't get how. Sit down, you really are new at this. You want some advice? Try working on the whole short fuse thing."

"I was a cop. A good cop. I'm good at what I do. I just don't do this kind of thing." Cal replied indignantly at Cole's seeing right through her.

"Let's start over. What have you got? How long's the kid, what's her name, been missing?"

"Her name is Mei. She's nearly blind. She's been gone since yesterday morning. Her mother knows she wasn't snatched because some of her clothes are gone, and a bunch of granola bars and stuff are missing."

"Arguments lately? They make her mad?"

"Nothing like that. She left for school like normal." Cal shrugged.

"Did they call the school?"

"Didn't show."

Cole had no idea how to help. He was grasping at straws. Little did California Corwin know he could use her help himself. Who was she anyway?

"How do you get a moniker like California?" Cole decided to change the subject for a moment and try to regroup.

"You mean how did a half-Asian Jewish girl get stuck with such a goofy name?"

"Ya, well, kind of." Cole gave her a grin.

"Hippies. My folks, were flower children from the east coast and California was the Garden of Eden. So..."

"Got it. So the 'Personal Investigations' thing, how long have you been in that game?" Cole wondered how a woman who needed his help finding a Special Needs kid got to be a glorified private eye.

"I was a cop. Military Police, then SFPD when I got out. Then this..." Cal pulled her hair back exposing the scar Cole had already noticed. "I sort of got retired."

"So what's that all about?' Cole said indicating the scar that ran from in front of her ear to below her collar.

"I was on patrol and my partner and I got a call. I went when I should have stayed. Bomb goes off and I get the boot for not following orders." Cal shrugged. "My partner's alive. I really don't know anything but law enforcement and thought the PI thing might be the next best thing."

"How's that working out? Fine. 'Til now. I don't even know where to start. I've never even talked to a retarded kid before, ya know? Do they think like normal people? Bet not." Cal was letting her guard down and her politically correct, professional facade was starting to collapse.

"How'd you get the case?"

"Chinese. Like I said, small community. They want to keep it contained."

"Then I guess why comes next. If this isn't your normal line..."

"I figured it was a way of, how'd you say it? Breach the wall?" Cal cut in.

"Good plan," Cole said flatly. "I tell you what. I'll talk to my editor here and at least keep it out of this paper.

But, I'm telling you, you need to call in the police. I have a friend, a lieutenant, Leonard Chin, he knows the community he could..."

"Hates me."

"Great. Well, call me old fashioned, but the cops have the cars, the radios, APBs, stuff like that," Cole said raising his eyebrows.

"Look, I get it. I told the parents the same thing, they said for me to do all I could for at least forty-eight hours. I got twenty-four left." Cal stood and extended her hand to Cole. "Maybe next time."

"I really do wish I had something for you, but this Amber Alert stuff, you know?" Cole said, standing and taking Cal's hand.

"Mr. Sage, a Lieutenant Chin on the phone for you," Hannah said from the door, waste paper basket still in her hand.

"I better take that."

"Yeah, thanks," Cal replied.

"Sage." Cole raised his hand palm out in good-bye.

"Cole, are you still working on the Parade piece?"

"Yeah, what up?"

"This is getting really weird. It's going to a level we're not used to. Got time for coffee?"

"Sure, where?"

Ten minutes later, Cole entered the Starbucks across from the Chinatown Gate. Leonard Chin was sitting toward the back by the window. Cole ordered a Mocha Venti and took a seat across from Chin.

"What's up?"

Chin turned his phone toward Cole.

"Jaime Rojas, street punk, 22nd Street Locos wanna be,

no record to speak of, stupid kid stuff mostly. Found him this morning like this."

Cole winched and said, "Are those real?"

"Yep, black as night and real, real deep. They've tattooed his forehead and the top of both hands. FCBZ big as would fit. I have seen some things, but this is just..." Chin's voice trailed off.

"The Firecracker Boyz are just a bunch of hoods. This is beyond just turf stuff. This is like crazy. It's like they are intentionally trying to start World War III with these guys."

"I haven't told you the best part. This kid was handcuffed to a streetlight, feet and hands, in the middle of Chinatown with a plastic bag around his neck. Now here's the best part, in the bag was a pistol, a .38, and I'm betting it is one of the ones used in the parade shootings. Now get this," Chin was showing a level of animation Cole hadn't seen in a long while, "the thing is, the only prints on the gun are Rojas's. And, we had him in the downtown lockup that day."

"So, he wasn't at the parade," Cole interjected.

"Exactly."

"What's the kid told you?"

"Nothing. He's in the hospital. They beat the shit out of him before the artwork. He's pretty bad off. I tell you Cole, these guys either aren't playing by the rules on purpose, or don't know what they are. Either way, we have a powder keg about to blow. I'm guessing the Mexicans don't know about this yet. When they do, there'll be hell to pay."

Chin's phone vibrated on the table, "Chin." The detective looked at Cole as he listened to the voice on the other end of the call, "Yeah, I figured as much. OK, thank you, Paul."

"Ballistics got a match. Same gun that killed the woman from Merced."

"But, Rojas wasn't the shooter," Cole groaned.

"Nothing about this whole thing makes sense. You saw a lot of gang stuff in Chicago, you ever seen anything like this?"

"No, you're right this is on a whole other level. Black gangs in Chicago, love to just shoot it out like cowboys. This is some kind of head game. But, I just don't think these clowns are that smart. This is just mean."

"You know the FCBZ?"

Cole realized he said too much. His meeting with Trick and his crew had to be kept under wraps, at least for now. "By reputation."

"Cole?" the barista called.

"Yeah." Cole stood to get his coffee.

When Cole returned to the table Chin was on the phone again. All this information was good. Was it meant for print, or was Chin just giving him more background? Cole sipped his coffee and waited.

"So how's the kid settling in?" Chin said laying down the phone.

"Good, good. I sent him out on an assignment. I can't wait to see what he comes up with." Cole's guilt at lying to his friend hung like a wet terrycloth robe on his conscience.

"Good kid. I like him."

"Me too. So, what of this info can I use, and what do I keep quiet?"

"Whatever. I don't think keeping this quiet matters anymore. If you or the kid turn up anything give me a call though."

"I don't get it. Why don't you just round up these FCBZ guys and give then the third degree."

"No witnesses, no finger prints, no snitches, no nothin'. A tattoo is clever but it can't be tied directly to any one person. We Chinese can be very tight lipped, you know. These guys won't talk. If anybody in Chinatown saw or heard anything they sure as hell won't talk after seeing what those guys did to that poor Mexican kid."

"What about the real bad guys? The Tongs?" Cole asked.

"It's a nice distraction for them. We're too busy dealing with gang foolishness to have time to dig in their backyard. The Tongs are so deep in the fiber of Chinatown we just don't have the time or money for them. The Chinese street gangs are just a nuisance. The Tongs usually keep them in check for the most part. Until this. This isn't normal. They'll screw up and then we'll get them. I just want it to be sooner rather than later," Chin sighed deeply. "Dǎjí fànzuì de yāo jiǎo de gōngzuò shì yǒngyuǎn zuò bù wán de."

"Alright Captain Canton, I give up."

"A crime fighter's job is never done." Leonard stood and with a typical swagger, gave Cole a sweeping salute and headed for the door.

"Later," Cole said without turning.

The street was nearly empty. Too early for the tour buses and the chill in the air wasn't very inviting, even for the locals. Cole sipped his Mocha and walked under the Chinatown gate. A few merchants swept the sidewalk in front of their shops, all the restaurants were still closed, and Cole felt as if he had the whole place to himself.

The girl who sold Cole his oranges the day before was

putting bananas into place on a green bin. She was bundled up in a hooded sweatshirt under a jacket all topped off with her green apron.

"How's grandpa?"

"He's in the back room by the heater." She giggled.

"Things are sure quiet around here," Cole said and took a sip of his coffee.

"People are staying in more." The girl took the lid off another box of bananas. "Those boys you went with came back here later. They told me to keep my mouth shut. They try to scare everybody. They think they're tough. I told them I would talk to whoever I wanted."

"You should be careful. Those guys are kind of crazy."

"Just stoners. They should worry about who they threaten. My grandfather is a "Shòu bǎohù de rén", a protected man. He's a friend of many members of the Ghee Cow Tong. He is not a member, but they respect him from boyhood. Old school Chinatown stuff, but still a force to be feared."

"Did you hear about the boy they found cuffed to the lamppost this morning? They were stupid enough to do that," Cole replied.

"That was a gang thing." The girl handed Cole an apple. "I went to school with all those losers. Fire Cracker Boys, duds if you ask me. If they walk with the ducks, soon they waddle like them. They'll all be dead or in jail sooner or later. Sad, but they choose their own path."

Cole rubbed the apple on his jacket shoulder and took a bite. "You're pretty fatalistic for someone so young."

"No, I am a realist. I'm going to USF, I'll get my degree. I'll always love Chinatown, but I won't always live here. I want to teach Women's Literature at a college back east somewhere."

"That's a goal well worth achieving and I think you're just the person to do it. I'm Cole by the way."

"I'm Mindy."

"What do I owe you for the apple?"

"On the house. But don't tell grandfather!" They both laughed.

There was an awkward silence. Thankfully, for Cole, his cellphone rang.

"I'll see you soon." He smiled at Mindy and indicated the phone.

"Cole Sage."

"Hey, remember me?"

"Yes, I do. Kelly, I'm so sorry I haven't called you." Cole winched.

"I've got you now! What's going on?" Kelly sounded upbeat but concerned.

"Way too much to talk about on the phone. I'm in Chinatown. On the street. I'm on my way back to the office. Can we please have dinner?"

"Please? Cole are you alright? You're worrying me." Kelly was calm, but in full protection mode.

"I'm fine, sweetheart. There's," just then the beep for an incoming call sounded. Cole looked at the display. It read 'Anthony Perez'.

"Kell, I'll have to call you back. There is an urgent call on the other line. Cole didn't wait for a response.

"Anthony!"

"You wish."

"Who is this?" Cole demanded.

"Mr. Zhuó."

"Trick?" Cole was not about to call him 'Mr. Zhuó'."

"Your Beaner is cluttering up my back room. When are you going to get my cousin's killer out of jail?"

"Things are in the works."

"I think you need to put pressure on your 'workers'."
Trick sounded more ominous than Cole remembered.

"Next time we talk I want to know when and where."

"I'm working on it. I am warning you. Nothing had
better happen to Anthony. I will burn Chinatown down
to get you. Is that clear enough for you?" Cole's vehemence
came from a dark place Cole tried to keep under lock but
the chains were broken and Zhuó got the message.

"You sound like a badass, old man. I don't scare easy."

"I think you do," Cole growled.

"Yeah, right." Zhuó's voice showed that the fierceness
in Cole's anger had hit home. The swagger and cool was
gone, and the person Cole now heard was vulnerable.

Without a thought, Cole hit the 'End' button and
Zhuó was gone. If he had any qualms about calling Luis,
they were gone now.

When the faded green 1983 Buick LeSabre pulled onto
the Bay Bridge, the man in the toll booth didn't even look
up. Luis Hernandez and his three friends made the trip
from East Los Angles in near-record time. Stopping only
once for gas and burgers, the four men cruised at a steady
seventy miles per hour. Cruise control, a good heater, and
a below average stereo made the trip almost bearable. I-5
traffic was light and they saw only one Highway patrol car,
and he was headed the other way.

They knew what they had to do. They would do it
quickly with as few casualties a possible, and would be
back on the road. Each of the men knew Whisper, they all
came up together, and they had all seen street action to-

gether. Though not claiming Norteño allegiance they were known and respected in the community. This was in part Whispers doing. He kept his crew in check and off other gang's turf and out of their business enterprises.

Before leaving L.A., Luis had made a call to a cousin who gave him the name of a solid San Francisco homie. Everything was prepared. Luis carried an untraceable burner phone that would be used twice. One call to Cole Sage, and one call to "Big Head" Ruelas, though Luis would address him as Jorge. One the way back the burner would get tossed off the bridge.

In the trunk of the Buick were four baseball bats, a length of pipe, rope, duct tape, and a can of black spray paint. Luis and Chuy Saldana were the only ones caring weapons. 9mm automatics taken from two 124th St Crips by Luis' cousin's crew. Untraceable and completely disposable.

Luis didn't like guns. He preferred box cutters. Up close, in your face. He could open a jugular vein or leave a gaping hole exposing intestines in a breath of a moment. The thing he liked about the razor blade, it was clean. As a teen, Luis used his first box cutter on a kid in his gym class. Not deep, nowhere significant, just a small cut really. The boy made a remark about Luis' gym socks not matching. Other kids in gym laughed and made Luis feel foolish.

After school, Luis walked past the boy in the crowed hall and cut him in the back of the arm midway between shoulder and elbow. Their eyes met. The boy never spoke or looked at Luis again.

Luis Alphonso Hernandez, was the fourth son of Antonio and Maria Hernandez. Undocumented aliens who met in the desert of Baja California. Together with twelve other people they crossed the border with only a plastic water jug and the clothes on their backs. Maria was alone and Antonio felt protective of her when the others disappeared into the darkness outside of Jacumba Hot Springs. The pair had stood alone on a dark stretch of road just across the border. Antonio reached out and took Maria's seventeen year old hand. They have been together ever since.

Their fourth son was a quite boy and well behaved. When the time came, like his brothers, he became an altar boy at St. Joseph's Catholic Church. The church was less than a mile from the Hernandez home, and Luis was proud that his parents trusted him to go back and forth alone. Luis took great pride in fulfilling his duties at the church and was especially proud when Father Chabot had chosen him over one of the older boys to carry the processional cross.

St Joseph's was in a rough neighborhood, and the new fair-skinned priest was something of a novelty in the Hispanic Barrio. He came from a small town in Iowa and was very fond of the children of the parish. He often referred to the altar boys as "his angels".

Over those next few months there was a change in Luis. His grades in school began to drop. His brother reported to his parents that Luis was smoking. This is not unheard of in the seventh grade, but it was in the Hernandez household. His father said he was "pasando por una fase" or "just going through a phase". His mother knew better. Something was wrong with her hijo mio.

Just before Christmas, as preparations were being made for all of the seasonal festivities and services, Father

Chabot disappeared. There was a lot of whispering among the mothers of the parish, and especially the mothers of the altar boys.

Orlando Melo began to miss a lot of school around Thanksgiving. He took longer than usual in the shower and had asked that his hair be buzzed short. This was an odd request his father thought, because he always took great care to see that his hair was just right before leaving for school.

On the sixteenth day of the Advent calendar, while doing the laundry, Orlando's mother spotted blood on his underwear. There were cordovan spots on three pairs of his shorts in the week's wash. His mother went to talk to Orlando. At first he said he "wiped too hard". Orlando could not look at his mother. As they sat on the edge of his bed, his mother gently stroking his back, Orlando began to cry. He was ashamed to be crying at twelve years old, but the tears flowed and his thin frame shook.

"What is it mijo? What has happened?"

Orlando could not say the words in English, he was too ashamed. Instead he whispered to his mother, "me ha tocado en mis lugares privados." *He touched me in my private places.*

They both wept and the story slowly came out how the Anglo priest chose Orlando as his "special angel". Later that night Orlando's mother lay in bed, darkness hiding her tears, and told her husband Jesus what had happened to their son.

Orlando's father was not a man of the church. Jesus Melo was a blasphemer and a violent, angry man. He had served two years in prison for assault. His wife was sure the "extra money" he brought home from time to time came from El Escorpiones Morenos, a violent group of old school gangsters in the barrio. She never asked and he never offered an explanation for the little extras the money provided.

Jesus was hard but fair with his children, and he was especially proud of his only son, Orlando. The news of his violation did not sit well. For several days, Jesus wore a scowl that seemed to take the light out of the room. He spoke little and could not look at Orlando.

The mothers of the St. Joseph's altar boys held close Orlando's secret. One by one, however, they confronted their sons. Some gently, some in hysterical tirades and accusations.

When Maria Hernandez sat across the kitchen table from Luis, her tears ripped open his heart. She spoke softly. Her love seemed to bleed from her very soul with each teardrop. She assured her son that there was no blame. There was no shame. If he had been touched, it was not the fault of God or the Holy Virgin. It was Satan himself.

Luis looked deep into his mother's eyes. In a voice strange to her, the voice of a man, her beloved son said to her, "If he had touched me this way, I would have slit his throat."

In that moment, Maria Hernandez knew her son had fallen victim to the priest's lust.

On Christmas Eve, Luis was awakened to the sound of voices coming from the front room. It was late and he thought the house was down for the night. He quietly left his warm bed and made his way down the hall. He dared not go into the living room or be seen. He recognized the voice that spoke to his father in a drunken slur. Manny Covarrubias worked with his father at the machine shop.

Gray haired, hard as steel, Manny was a charter member of Escorpiones Morenos. He was very drunk and very loud.

"Manny, you need to go home. Tomorrow is Christmas," Antonio pleaded.

"There is something you must know. It is a very big secret. But you need to know. For your boy, for Luis." Manny's voice dropped to a hoarse whisper.

"OK. Then you must go home. It's late."

"You know I love you, Antonio. Te quiero, mi mejor amigo."

"Yes, we have been friends a very long time. What is this secret?" Antonio was concerned because of Luis' name being mentioned.

"That faggot priest. He is on his way to China. Ese pedazo de mierda."

"What do you mean?"

"Jesus Melo and some of the Escorpiones made sure he will not come back."

"What are you saying Manny?" Antonio was not sure what you called this kind of sin.

"Eight pieces. Eight containers. All on their way to China. Each with a piece of that pedophile priest inside the scrap metal."

"Oh sweet Christ," Antonio said softly.

"But it is a secret. Oh, and he won't be going with his dick. Jesus fed it to that pit bull of his while the priest watched. Funny, eh?" Manny laughed hoarsely.

"OK amigo, I will keep the secret. But you really must go."

"I just had to give you this Christmas gift. If he did touch Luis, he's paid for it."

"Yes, he has. Goodnight." Antonio said, opening the front door.

"Feliz Navidad, Tonio."

"Feliz Navidad."

The front door closed and Luis slipped back to his bed. This is how problems are solved. From that day forward, Luis never went to church. The priest hurt him, but he hurt his mother more, and that was unforgiveable. Luis Hernandez' heart turned to ice, he was a man to be feared.

EIGHT

415 McClarren made many strange noises for an empty building. It seemed to groan and stretch like an old man getting up from his chair. Marco woke first. He lay silently next to Mei and listened to her breathing. He listened to the sounds of the building coming from above and below him. It was his building.

As he lay staring at the ceiling, his stomach growled and gurgled. Marco became more and more impatient with his sleeping friend. He was hungry and he want to get something to eat. Rolling away from where Mei still slept, Marco quietly moved to the break room.

He opened the refrigerator and got two tamales. From the counter he took two granola bars and two juice boxes and placed them on the table.

He stood studying the microwave above the stove a long moment before opening the door.

"Hmmm, this is not like my house."

Marco laid the two tamales on the glass wheel, closed the door, and hit the square with the "2". The light came on and the wheel began to turn.

"Yessss!" Marco said triumphantly, pumping his fists in the air.

As the microwave hummed, Marco opened drawer after drawer looking for a plate or fork. Across from the microwave, on the opposite wall, he found a small paper bag with a half dozen plastic spoons, knives, and forks. He took the bag and placed it on the counter next to the granola bars.

The ding of the microwave sent Marco happily back to where Mei was still sleeping.

"Gooood Moorning!" Marco sang. "Good morning to you!"

Mei rolled over and felt around on the floor for her glasses.

"Are you hungry?" Marco beamed. "I have breakfast ready for you."

Mei sat up and adjusted her glasses. "Yes, I am hungry.

"It is all ready and on the table in the kitchen.

"You are sure nicer than my brother!" Mei giggled.

"Really? I wish I had a brother."

"My brother is a bad boy. He makes my father very mad all the time," Mei began.

"Why?"

"He took money from my father's desk at his office. He took money from my mama's purse. He said he didn't, but nobody believes him because he is always such a big liar."

Marco offered Mei his hand and helped her get up from the floor.

"What did he buy?" Marco asked.

"Drugs. He always uses drugs. He told me I should get high with him. He said it would make me see better. See what a liar he is."

"What is 'get high'?" Marco asked.

"I don't know for sure. It is what drugs do. I heard my parents yelling at him one night when he got home. He told them they were old and didn't know about what's good."

"That make you sad?" Marco asked as they moved into the break room.

"A lot. He used to be nice to me and nice to my parents. He's a Firecracker Boy."

"That sounds fun. I like firecrackers!" Marco perked up with the excitement of fireworks.

"Not that kind, you silly. He's a gangbanger."

"Like the guys in red?"

"Yes, except they just have hats. They look silly to me. Their t-shirts are so big."

"You know a lot of stuff. I don't know stuff like you."

"I just know he's a bad kid. He tells my parents he's not a gangster but I saw his hat one day when I went by his room. He was hiding it, but I saw him."

"I have a Giants hat. I left it at home," Marco bragged.

"I got an idea. Let's eat and look out the window. Mei smiled.

"OK."

The pair picked up their tamale, granola bar and juice box and went to the reception area. They chose a desk by a window and hopped up on it and put their food between them. All settled and admiring the view, they began unwrapping and eating.

They sat for a long time looking out the window and eating their tamales in silence. Marco softly thumped his heels on the front of the desk. Mei looked out the window at the seagulls, seemingly motionless as they floated, wings spread on the wind, outside the fourteenth floor.

Marco stopped bumping the desk and Mei stared at the door. They sat perfectly still leaning toward the sound beyond the door. Down the hall a door slammed. Moments later another.

"Someone's coming," Marco whispered.

"What should we do?" Mei replied.

Before they could decide, a voice came from beyond the door.

"Do we have to check every damn door in this building?" a man said loudly.

From a distance another man answered, "Can't have squatters."

The first man was even closer as he said, "Why do you think there's squatters?"

"The back door was open." The second man was now louder than before.

Marco couldn't breathe. Mei held him tight by the arm. The doorknob shook, but the door didn't open.

"This one's locked!"

"Wish they all were. Can't get in a locked door. OK, let's go."

As the voices of the two men gradually faded, Marco sucked in a deep breath.

"Who locked the door?"

"I guess I did. I was trying out the button." Marco shrugged.

"We are soooo lucky!" Mei squealed.

"I hope they don't come back again," Marco said worriedly.

"Me too."

Kelly was waiting at a table near the window when Cole arrived at Vicoletto's. He couldn't find a place to park on Green Street, so he parked around the corner. Her hair looked beautiful tied in a bright red and white silk scarf. She smiled and waved and Cole saw she wore lipstick to match. *How did I get so lucky*, Cole thought, as Kelly stood to give him a peck on the cheek.

"Mrs. Mitchell, you look absolutely ravishing!" Cole's compliment sounded more like bragging than a compliment.

"Why thank you, sir," Kelly said reaching across the table and taking both Cole's hands. "I'm worried about you. Don't lie, there is something eating you, and you need to let it out."

"Man, it is so good to be with you. It seems like a year," Cole sighed.

"It's been three days. Don't change the subject."

"How about we talk while we eat? I'm starving."

The waiter's timing was perfect. He seemed to slide up next to the table."

"Hey Johnny, I got this!" a booming voice came from behind the waiter. He bowed and slipped away.

"Sal!" Kelly said with smile.

"Ma che bella signorina Kelly! Who'sa this ugly brute?"

"No tip for you, Sal."

"Just a joke, Mr. Newspaperman! What? You can't take a joke no more?"

"Of course he can. What wonderful thing do you have for me tonight?" Kelly charmed.

"For you, Sautéed prawns and cherry tomato brandy cream sauce." Sal bowed his head ever so slightly.

"Fantastico!"

"And for you, Mr. Cole, Lobster Ravioli, your favorite." Sal slapped Cole on the shoulder. "I know, I know, lots and lots of parmesano."

"Love ya, Sal," Cole said, grinning up at Sal.

Sal made his way back to the kitchen and Cole snapped a bread stick in half.

"Here you go." He offered.

"No more stalling. You have never before in your life said can we 'please' have dinner. Please. I know something is wrong. How can I help? You need a hug?" Kelly gave a soft laugh.

"You remember me telling you about Whisper Lopez? Anthony Lopez, the kid I gave Ellie's Scholarship to? He surprised me the day of Chris's funeral. He is my new intern."

"Isn't it working out?"

"No, no it's not that. There is a problem. A big problem. Listen, Kelly, I'm really serious. You cannot tell a soul what I'm about to tell you. I don't want any Kellyisms. I need to tell somebody. I need to tell you because I love you and I trust you." Cole looked at his napkin.

"Did you just say you loved me?" Kelly's face seemed to radiate light. Her smile looked like a kid who just got her first bike, or a dad whose kid just hit his first home run.

Cole looked up into her eyes and nearly wept. She was the most beautiful thing he had ever seen. In his deep despair and worry, he said the words he'd been dying to say, and they just came out. He'd been waiting for a special moment. This certainly wasn't what he had in mind.

"I guess I did." Cole smiled.

"I love you too, Cole Sage."

They sat for a long moment holding each other's hands across the table.

"Whatever you have to tell me, can you wait a bit? I just want to..." Kelly's voice trailed off.

"If I'd known I would get this reaction, I wouldn't have waited so long." Cole gave a self-conscious grin.

"Antipasto," Waiter Johnny said, setting the plate awkwardly beside their clasped hands.

Neither one of them looked up.

"Kiss me," Kelly whispered.

Cole rose from his chair, leaned across the table and gently kissed Kelly's crimson lips.

"Straciatella," once again the waiter's timing was awful, but the soup looked delicious.

"Would you like to try again?" Kelly giggled.

"The kiss or the story?"

"Maybe the story, I think another kiss might cause a scene."

"Anthony has been abducted." Cole just dove in head first. "I sent him to get some background on the reaction in Chinatown about the parade shootings and the Firecracker Boyz snatched him." Cole sighed deeply. The relief of saying it out loud was an almost physical weight lifted from him.

"Cole," Kelly said softly.

"I didn't know what happened until I went to Chinatown the next morning asking around. The next thing I know I'm in the little Dim Sum joint across a table from the little punk who has him."

"Have you called the police?"

"No."

"Why not, for heaven's sake?"

"These are unthinking, uncaring gangbangers. They will kill him in the blink of an eye and dump him in the Bay." Cole paused. "Here's the thing. Anthony came from that life. He knows who these guys are and how they work. Cops will get him killed. I know it, he knows it, they know it."

"What are you going to do?" Kelly interrupted.

"I already did it. That's what's gnawing at me."

"For the lady!" Sal stood at the end of the table. "What'sa matta? You don't like the soup?"

They hadn't touched the soup or the antipasto. Kelly looked up and winced. Cole reached for his spoon.

"We were so busy talking, we forgot. Not forgot, just..." Kelly picked up her spoon.

Sal set the plate of prawns in front of Kelly. Cole moved his soup bowl over and made space for the ravioli.

"Try to remember this is on the table, eh?" Sal walked away, obviously miffed.

Cole exhaled hard and his lips kind of flapped. "I called Anthony's old number-two man, Luis. He will be here in San Francisco any time now. He's coming to get Anthony back."

"I'm not sure what you're saying."

"He's kind of a psychopath."

"Meaning?"

"He will do whatever it takes. He saved me from probably getting really hurt, if not killed."

"How?" Kelly wasn't smiling. She was showing no emotion at all.

"He sliced a man's head front to back with a box cutter until his partner let me go."

"And you called *him* for help?"

"Yep."

"Why?"

"Like the man said, 'don't bring a knife to a gun fight'. This guy is fearless and lethal. He will get Anthony back. The gangs will keep killing each other and Anthony will be alive."

"But at what cost?" Kelly said leaning forward, her brow furrowed in concentration.

"Whatever it takes."

Kelly picked up her fork and began eating her prawns. She didn't look up and Cole couldn't even tell if she was breathing. She took a drink of water and took a long deep breath though her nose.

"He means that much to you?"

"I have invested nearly five years in him. He is a journalist, or will be, because of me. He is the phoenix that rose from Ellie's ashes, so to speak. Yes, he means that much to me." Cole sat straight and cleared his throat. He was resolute in his decision. He told the woman he loved. Her reaction would cement or destroy their relationship.

Kelly looked down at the floor next to their table, then up, and met Cole's eyes. "I can't say I approve of what these men may do. I don't know how their world works. Thanks be to God I have lived a pretty sheltered life. But, if I am going to love you, I have to trust you. I have to believe that you would protect me, no matter what it took." I love you Cole, and you have made the best call you know how to make. But I swear, if you end up behind bars, I am not going to be happy!" Kelly gave him one of her 100 watt smiles and poked another prawn with her fork.

"Pssst. I love you!" Cole whispered.

NINE

Jorge Ruelas answered on the third ring. The sound of machinery in the background made it difficult for Luis to hear Jorge's thin reedy voice.

"This is Hernandez," Luis said loudly.

"I can hear you homie. No need to shout. Damn, I be deaf."

"You got something for me?" Luis lowered his voice. "Ready to go."

Ruelas gave him the directions to his shop. Luis ended the call without saying a word. One call down.

Tiko's Paint and Body Shop looked like a thousand others. San Francisco style was a bit more cramped than LA, but the signs were all the same. Half-finished Bondo covered cars, primered windowless vehicles with for sale signs, and shiny, freshly painted cars waiting to be picked up lined the street in front of the yard.

"Shitty painter," Luis said to Chuy, as they walked past a finished car. "Look at the overspray."

"You could give 'em lessons, Holmes." The men laughed as they walked into the fenced in yard.

A man approached the pair a few yards inside the gate. He wore a greasy, Oakland Raiders t-shirt and jeans. His arms, neck, and face were covered in faded, green-hued jail tattoos. Above his right eye read XIV. Under the same eye were three tear drops. If this was the face of customer relations, it was not like a thousand other body shops.

"We're here to see Ruelas," Luis spoke first trying to show dominance.

"He know you're coming?"

"Where is he?"

Luis would not answer questions. He saw and treated this flunky as an inferior and would deal with him as little as possible.

The man knew he was dealing with someone he needed to show respect. He turned, and took about ten steps before shouting, "Big Head!"

From one of the open bays a tall, fair-skinned Latino appeared. He wore baggy blue jeans and a khaki work shirt.

"Luis?" said the reedy voice from the phone.

"Hey!" Luis smiled in greeting.

The two clasped hand and gave each other a one-armed hug.

"How's that réprobos primo tuyo?" Ruelas asked, with a wide grin.

"He told me to kick your ass," Luis replied.

"Only because he can't do it!" Ruelas laughed.

"Prob lee."

"Lemme show you what we got."

As Ruelas led the way, it was apparent where he got his nickname. He possessed a cranium that looked half again larger than a head should be for such a tall slender man. He took Luis and Chuy to the last work bay of the four lining the building. Inside was a dark green Toyota Corolla with tinted windows and very little chrome.

"Ruelas reached through the open driver window and removed the keys and a piece of paper from under the visor.

"Here you go, clear as crystal and phony as hell," Ruelas said, handing Luis a pink slip and keys to the Toyota. "Got one for me?"

"Signed sealed and delivered," Luis said, taking a similar document from is shirt pocket.

"Then we're done. Leave the keys under the floor mat."

Jorge "Big Head" Ruelas turned and walked back toward the front of the building. Luis and Chuy looked at each other and shrugged.

"Tell your cousin we're even," Ruelas said over his shoulder without breaking stride.

The Corolla was smaller, but the stereo was nicer than the Buick's. Chuy started the car and pulled out into the yard. The tattooed man watched them from the side until they were out the gate.

Luis tossed the key to the Buick to Juan Lopez, Anthony's second cousin, and told him to put them under the driver's side mat. Juan and Carlos Prasado, the fourth member of the crew, got in the back of the Toyota. They drove away and didn't look back.

At eight-thirty, Cole's cell phone rang. He had been sitting in the dark waiting for the call. Kelly went to watch

Jennie while Erin and Ben went for a late super with friends. Cole fumbled for the phone.

"Sage," He said on the third ring.

"We're here."

"That took a while."

"I had business," Luis stated flatly. "Tomorrow at noon, meet us at the Fisherman's Wharf sign."

"Us?"

"You didn't think I would come alone did you?"

"Guess not," Cole said.

The line went dead.

Hannah was standing behind Cole's desk when he arrived. There were neat stacks of folders on his desk. Each stack was labeled with a post-it note, each note contained a bold message in bold black sharpie: FILE? TRASH? ARE YOU KIDDING ME? WTH?

Hannah looked up as Cole stopped in the doorway of his office.

"I know they say a cluttered desk is the sign of a clever mind, or some such nonsense. But no one can work with this much crap under their nose." Hannah waved her arms over the four stacks on the desk. "I've done the hard part. You need to decide what's what. Toss, file or whatever, I'll do it, but for goodness sake we cannot work like this.

"Well, alright! Good morning to you too!" Cole put his hands up palms out in surrender.

"Too brusque?"

"No. No, I'm just not used to having anybody care if this door is open or shut. Thank you. I have been a bit out of sorts lately."

"I heard about the editor's partner. Did you know him?"

"Not in the Biblical sense, but we were friends," Cole laughed. "He would have liked that joke."

"Messages." Hannah pointed at three pink message slips impaled on a very spiked memo holder. Hanna responded to Cole's inquisitive look with, "Ebay. I got thinking it would come in handy. Six bucks. I think it's really old."

"Would you like a cup of coffee?" Cole asked.

"Why do you?" Hanna replied.

"No, I heard it makes hyper people mellow out sometimes."

"Too much?"

"No, I'm just feeling my way." Cole moved to one of the chairs in front of his desk and sat down. "Have a seat."

"Here?" Hanna asked.

"Sure. why not?"

"You said you want something important to do. What was it you said about not just filing and answering phones? I got something for you. But first, a few ground rules." Cole waited for a response.

"OK".

"First, what we do stays in this office. No matter how small or insignificant. I will, whenever possible, give you the hows and whys of what I ask you to do. Sometimes I won't."

"Any problem with that?"

"Loose lips sink ships," Hanna said brightly.

"Exactly. I don't trust anybody. I want to trust you." He paused as Hanna grinned anxiously. Cole continued. "We'll see. Here's what I want to you do. Find out everything you can on a fella named Zhuó, I don't have a first name. And a Chinese business man named Cheung Chou."

"How do you spell..."

"Figure it out. In the basement there is a kid that is on our team. Tell him you work with me and he will be a great help if you get stuck. But, make sure you have done everything you know to do first or he'll make you feel like an idiot. He has me. His name is Randy Callen. Good guy, but a bit of a show off. OK, are we good?"

"When you say 'everything'," Hanna paused. "Do you mean, everything?"

"Like, do we break the rules a bit?"

"Sort of."

"If need be, shred them. Is that a problem?"

"Is that legal?"

"You have a problem with doing a little cyber skullduggery? Say so now. If you are really on board, buckle up. We play hard, fast, and some would say real loose with the rules. I'm so-so with it. I turn a blind eye. Randy gets off on it. Where do you fit in? In or out?"

"In like Flynn!" Hanna's eyes sparkled with excitement.

"How old are you? Never mind. Reference understood, and appreciated."

Hanna stood to her feet. She started to speak and thought better of it. As she made her way around the desk she gave Cole a nod. "I'll have it for you yesterday. Thanks."

Cole just shook his head and gave a little chuckle.

A thin man in a suit several sizes too big, covered in silver paint from head to foot, stood on a pedestal still as a statue.

Or rather, he wants you to think he is still as a statue. The careful observer sees slight movement and his eyes dart around the crowd. When the occasional child would toss a coin in his silver coffee can, the silver man would tip his hat and change positions. The crowd reacts with squeals from the children, and chuckles from the adults.

Luis and his three friends stood at the edge of the crowd watching the Anglos.

"I don't get it. Why would that fool spray paint his clothes and hat silver?" Chuy ask.

"Changos will do anything for a penny!"

The group burst into laughter. It was nearly noon, and Luis continuously scanned the sidewalk for Cole. The crowds flowed like rivers around them. A black man in a floppy hat played a keyboard to their right and sang into a makeshift PA system. His voice was strong and the beat up old speakers seemed pointless. Luis moved closer as he began to sing Donny Hathaway's "Where Is the Love?". It was his mother's favorite song. The old guy does a nice job, but he really needs a girl to sing Roberta Flacks part, Luis thought as he moved closer.

"Talented guy, huh?" Cole said over Luis' shoulder.

"Hey, old man!" Luis turned and gave Cole a smile.

Cole offered him his hand and to his surprise the big Mexican gave him a bear hug.

"It has been a long time. You're looking good. Got skinny on me. What, they don't feed you up here?" Luis laughed. "Come meet the crew."

As they approached the three men standing beneath the Fisherman's Wharf sign, Luis' demeanor changed. His relaxed attitude was gone and a tense hardness came over him.

"Chuy, Juan, Carlos, this is Cole Sage. He's a mouthy smart ass, but he's good people."

One by one Cole shook hands with the three men.

"You guys blend right in around here," Cole said, taking in their obviously recent purchases of "local apparel".

Chuy's hoody was emblazoned with "Alcatraz Psycho Ward Outpatient" across the front. Juan wore a San Francisco Forty-Niner's jersey and Carlos sported an Oakland A's yellow and green button up jersey. They looked every inch the tourist.

"So, can I buy you a cup of chowder or a shrimp cocktail?" Cole offered.

"Let's find a place to talk quiet." Luis said.

The five men walked away from the crowded sidewalk and across the parking lot to a row of benches next to the Franciscan restaurant. There were three sections of benches. Each faced the water with another bench that backed it, facing the small plaza next to the restaurant. Cole and Luis sat facing San Francisco Bay. Carlos and Juan sat with their backs to Luis and Cole. Chuy stood, leaning back on the chain link that bordered the plaza.

"Have you heard from the ones who have Whisper?" Luis began, as they sat down.

"Not since yesterday."

"You've seen these guys? You talk to them?" Luis asked.

"I went to Chinatown to see if anybody had seen or talked to Anthony. Two Firecracker Boyz confronted me and took me to a little restaurant. A guy they call Trick is the ringleader. He told me he had Anthony and wanted his cousin, who's in jail, in return." Cole paused and looked at Chuy, who was watching him closely. "He called yesterday around this time and said time was running out. Nothing since then."

"What makes him think you can get somebody out of jail?" Luis seemed bewildered.

"No clue. They're all late teens and early twenties. They reek of weed and are obviously wasted most of the time. But, they are insanely violent. I was there, at the parade. They just walked into the street and started shooting. No fear, no concern for the bystanders, it was crazy. I've never seen anything like it. The Norteños shot back, but they were playing defense. No excuse but..."

"Fools," Luis growled. "So what color do they claim?"

"None I can see. They dress in white tees and chinos and they wear white ball caps with FCBZ stitched in black and silver. Not hard to miss."

"So, if I go to Chinatown, I'll see these fools?"

"I imagine. They think they own the place."

"The thing I don't get, is why the cops don't have these guys locked up. I mean, they must have witnesses, yeah?"

"It gets back to the "all Asians look alike" and they all have an iron clad alibis. The merchants are so afraid of them, they all claim the guys were hard at work in their shops."

"So, we go get a couple and make our own trade." Luis stood up. "Chuy, you hungry?"

"Always."

"What you say we go get some Chinese?"

"Yeah, sounds good."

Juan and Carlos stood and came around to the chain link fencing. In jerseys and ball caps they looked less than threatening, but like a platoon of soldiers they were primed, ready, and just waiting for orders to march.

Cole was the last to stand. He wasn't quite sure what came next, or his part in it, if any. He stood silently waiting for Luis to say something to him.

"So, where you gonna be?" Luis finally asked.

"With you guys, of course," Cole replied.

"No. No, you're not getting anywhere near this shit."

"This is my fight too."

"Look, you got a good heart. This isn't your thing. One of two things gonna happen, you're gonna get killed, or hurt bad, or you're gonna get one of us hurt or killed. Which do you prefer?" Luis folded his arms and stared at Cole.

"Well, neither one, but..." Cole's voice showed he knew the argument was over. "So, what do you want me to do?"

"I gotta have someplace to bring Whisper. I don't think he will want to come home with us. Do you?"

The trio along the fence laughed. Luis shot them a look and the laughing stopped.

"I'll," Cole began but was interrupted by his phone. He looked at Luis.

"You gonna answer it?"

"Hello."

"I think you're a liar."

"Trick?" Cole pointed at the phone. Luis stepped closer.

"You said you would work on getting my cousin out of jail. I talked to him. He's heard nothing from anyone. You're stalling. What's your game? You want this Beaner with a bullet in his head?" Zhuó was not his usual smooth, controlled self. Could he be panicking? Cole thought.

"Say hello, Norteño Newsman." There was a brief pause, then a familiar voice, "Cole, screw this guy!"

"Anthony!"

Luis reached out and snatched the phone from Cole's hands. "You do tricks, puta?" Luis growled into the phone.

"Sage? Sage!" Zhuó yelled into the phone.

"No. I'm not Mr. Sage. You will be praying to Christ I was when I find you." Luis's voice was controlled and terrifying in its delivery. "Now listen close you slit eye cockroach. I am going to give you a chance to live. Let my hermano go free, and you and your little band of wannabes will be eating rice again tomorrow. If not, you will be coming back as dog, or whatever it is you people think you do."

"Ooo so scary. Go to hell or whatever it is you people think you do!" Zhuó laughed and the line went dead.

Luis handed Cole the phone. "I tried."

Cole could think of nothing to do but shrug his shoulders.

Without a word, the five men left the Franciscan plaza and crossed the parking lot back to the Fisherman's Wharf sign.

"Where are you parked?" Cole asked.

"Just off there." Chuy pointed.

The group walked a block up Taylor and turned on Beach. The dark green Corolla was parked on the curb, meter expired. A yellow envelope containing a parking ticket was under the windshield wiper.

"That's not good," Cole said pointing at the ticket. "That's a twenty-nine dollar fine."

Luis walked to the front of the car and gently took the ticket from the wiper and then tore in to a dozen pieces. "Let Big-Head pay it!"

Everyone laughed except Cole. He didn't get the joke.

"So, where do we drop Whisper off?" Luis asked.

"Safest place would be in front of The Chronicle. 901 Mission." Cole looked at the four men one by one. "What can I do?"

"Stay out of the way, old man." Luis gave Cole a grin,

but there was no mirth in his eyes. "We got this." Luis slapped Cole on the shoulder and opened the passenger door. "I'll call you."

"Luis, for God's sake don't kill anybody. We don't want that on Anthony's conscience." Cole cleared his throat. "Or yours."

The door closed and Juan and Carlos got in the back. Chuy already had the motor running. With a quick beep-beep of the horn, they pulled away from the curb. The blacked out windows kept Cole from seeing even a silhouette of the men in the car.

"Your friend is a racist," Zhuó said, turning to face Anthony.

"Cole? Not hardly," Anthony sneered.

"Not him, the Mexican."

"Mexican?" Anthony's mind raced. *Who is he talking about?*

"One of your brother Beaners. Sage put him on the phone. He was very disrespectful. He just got you killed, I think."

"And Beaner isn't racist?" Anthony asked.

"Maybe a little." Zhuó shrugged. "It won't be dark for a while, so you should maybe pray to the guy nailed up on the wood thing. You Christians are such a bloody religion. A bloody guy gets nailed to a, what do you call it? A cross! Then you pretend you're eating his body and drinking his blood. Does that make you cannibals, vampires, or both? Weird as hell, if you ask me." Zhuó shook his head.

"You know, belittling a person's religion is as bad as racism, maybe worse. Did you ever think about that?"

"I didn't."

Too many blunts probably to do much thinking past finding a lighter, huh?"

"I think you're going to be a smart ass right up until I put a bullet through your eye." Zhuó gave a chuckle. "I didn't know you tamale peelers were such a funny bunch. I mean other than the way you talk."

"You won't get the chance."

Anthony didn't bother to watch Trick Zhuó go back up the stairs. He was too busy trying to figure out who Cole had put on the phone. How did Trick know he was Mexican? Maybe he was just trying to rattle him. Maybe he made up the whole thing. What if he's not lying? Anthony's mind raced.

Would Cole dare call Luis? The last time they spoke it was very ugly. Luis' anger actually frightened Anthony. They had been friends as long as he could remember. They were closer than brothers, yet Luis said terrible things, cruel, hurtful things. At the time, Anthony was shocked but, when Luis began turning over tables, throwing bottles and glasses, Anthony turned and walked out. A bottle hit the door casing, narrowly missing Anthony's head, as he opened the door. That was the last time they spoke.

In the years since, many times Anthony intended to pick up the phone and call his old friend. But he never did. A lot of the personal hurt and anger that Luis felt was because Anthony, his only real friend, deserted him.

Luis is five years and 400 miles away. There is no way he would come to rescue him. Zhuó was lying.

He made his choice to go to college. It was either break free of the life he led or end up dead. The irony is that the gang life he broke free of was now about to kill him anyway.

Maybe it was time to say a prayer.

TEN

Three massive tour buses pulled into the bus lane, one after another, just to the west of the Chinatown gate. Forty or so camera-swinging tourists from eighteen to eighty hopped, eased, and were helped from the buses. One bus of Germans, one bus of Japanese, and one bus of Brazilians, who followed a yellow and green flag held high overhead by the young woman in the green pillbox hat and matching pant suit.

From across the street Luis and his friends watched patiently.

"Think we could fit in?" Luis asked.

"Except for the Portuguese." Carlos offered.

The group crossed the street and fell in line with the Brazilians. Staying in the back quarter of the group, no one seemed to even notice their presence. As they walked along, keeping their voices down, and smiling and nodding, their eyes never stopped scanning the sidewalk for white ball caps and tattooed Fire Cracker Boyz.

It didn't take long to find what they were looking for. The three FCBZ hats down the street might as well have been flashing neon signs. Luis and Juan slipped away from the group and began looking at the Chinatown souvenirs at Lee and Company. Chuy and Carlos went to the same side of the street as the three Asian gangsters.

The FCBZ crew stood smoking, chatting, and laughing at the curb next to an alley. Two of the young men were the same ones who had accompanied Cole to his meeting with Trick Zhou. The tallest of them seemed to be the leader of the group. He dominated the conversation, and was loud enough to be noticed by the groups as they passed in review. The jokes were rude, and directed at the tourists. Profanity laced their descriptions of men and women alike. Nothing seemed to be off limits. Height, weight, ample breast size or not, backsides, and bellies all drew the cruel and crass remarks from the trio.

As the Brazilian delegation moved up the sidewalk, Luis slipped back into the crowd. As he came within a few feet of the FCBZs, one fist bumped the others and broke from the group and walked straight toward Chuy and Carlos. Luis turned and crossed back across the street. As the lone Asian gangster passed Chuy and Carlos, they gave him a lead of a few feet and followed him toward the great green gate.

Juan and Luis followed from the other side of the street. Luis just a few feet behind Juan. Without eye contact or signals, the four men maneuvered in and out of the crowded sidewalks like a Blue Angels' maneuver. All four men joined ranks and passed through Chinatown Gate together. As luck would have it, their prey turned right and proceeded in the direction of their car.

Three car lengths from the Corolla, Juan and Luis passed the unsuspecting FCBZ. As they reached the front of the Corolla, they pivoted nearly in unison and faced Peter Lu.

Peter started to go around Juan's right but was stopped by a large arm across his chest. He tried to push Juan's arm away, but was met with a forceful forearm shove back to center.

"What the hell, man!" Peter shouted.

"Sshh." Luis put a finder to his lips. "Don't cause a fuss."

"What do want?" Peter tried to appear tougher than he was feeling.

"I'm feeling like Chinese take-out," Luis replied.

"You know who I am? I'm a Firecracker Boy. You need to just walk away." The slight quiver in Ricky's voice gave away his fear.

"He's kind of cute," Juan said with a smarmy grin.

"Reminders me of the big black guy's bitch in lock up. What they call him Lotus Petal?" Chuy laughed and gave Carlos a jab in the shoulder.

"You been in lock up?" Carlos said to Peter in an unfriendly tone.

"No. And I ain't goin'"

"You're right, because we're not cops," Luis said. "Let's go."

Chuy opened the back door to the Corolla and Carlos and Juan grabbed Peter Lu by the arms.

"Hey! Trick will kill you! FCBZ ain't no bitch."

"Trick? Now, that's an idea. If you give us any trouble,

we will find a nice big brotha looking for some exotic Asian boy for a night of oriental delights. This is San Francisco. Gay pride, all that." Luis put on his best pimp. It was so convincing even Carlos turned and looked. "We will turn you every way but loose."

"Especially out!" Chuy laughed. "Shut up and get in."

No effort was made to put his head down, just Juan's powerful shove into the back seat. Peter's head banged hard against the car.

"Good morning!" Hanna said brightly.

Cole looked up and for a moment forgot who his new secretary was. Somewhere on the streets of San Francisco were four very committed, extremely violent men, ready to do God-knows-what to get their friend back. Cole was just staring at his cell phone as if willing it to ring. The interruption brought him back to the reality of work, the office, and the woman standing in front of him with a blue file folder.

"Whatcha got?"

"Good morning to you too. You need coffee or something?"

Cole stood and reached out for the folder.

"This will take a bit of explaining." Hanna began. "Your friend in the basement really knows his stuff. Like you said, I'm not sure I want to know the "hows and whys" of his ability to get in places but he came up with some interesting stuff." Hanna opened the folder and began to read. "Cheung Chou, Miss Corwin's client, net worth 2.5 million. Owns, yada, yada, yada. OK here's the good stuff. On three separate occasions he has bailed his son, Ricky

Chou 18, out of jail. Then there is no record of the arrest, a court appearance, charges being dropped, nothing. How weird is that?"

"What'd the kid do?" Cole sat back down.

"Petty stuff mostly. Drunk in public, shoplifting, but, here's the biggie, street gang activity, strong-arm robbery, intimidation of a witness, possession of a firearm, and possession of a controlled substance with intent to sell."

"Go back to the gang stuff. What gang?"

"The Firecracker Boys, 'Boyz' with a z."

"The kid is connected to old school Chinatown money. How else could his arrest just disappear?" Cole could have cared less about the arrest; what he cared about was Luis and company walking into a well organized crime operation the size and strength of which the SFPD probably couldn't measure. "Have you called Corwin?"

"Not yet, I wasn't sure what or how much you wanted me to give her."

"Give her all of it. I'm not sure what value it is to her." Cole said flatly.

Hanna looked crest fallen. She turned and started back for her desk completely deflated.

"Hey," Cole called out.

Hanna turned slowly, "Yeah."

"Nice work. Thank Randy. You guys earned your keep for the month. Nice to have you on board." Cole smiled, sensing he had thanked her just in the nick of time. "Were you offering coffee earlier?"

"Yes! Coming right up!" the lights came back on in Hanna's eyes and she spun around, head up and shoulders back.

Cole had no way of reaching Luis. If the Chou kid was

connected to any of the Tongs, this just became way bigger that just getting Anthony back. The guys were going into a fight with an enemy using automatic weapons, carrying box cutters and a couple of pop guns.

Cole picked up the phone and punched in the number for Leonard Chin's cell.

"Cole, what's up?"

"Tell me about Cheung Chou."

"Really? Where this come from?"

"Trying to give a new friend a little help. You know him?" Cole wasn't giving anything he didn't have to.

"Never met him. His name comes up from time to time. He's one of those in-the-shadows Tong guys. Respect and privilege without getting his hands dirty."

Cole hesitated before his next question. "Connected enough to get his kid off two or three felony raps?"

"So, what is this really about?" Chin replied.

"Nothin' yet. Turning over a few rocks and some odd bugs are showing up."

"There have been rumors of deals and the occasional blind eye being turned to Chinatown crimes. Can you give me a for instance?"

"Not yet."

Chin cleared his throat. "I can see through you like cellophane, Sage. Listen to me. Leave these people alone. They have been playing their game for a hundred and fifty years. You, my friend, can begin to understand the rules. They can make irritations disappear and me, or anybody else, will ever know what happened. So, whatever it is you're sticking that nose of yours into, drop it. There are other Chinatown stories. The parade shooting wasn't Tong, I can guarantee you that. If somebody's kid was involved let us sort that out." Chin paused. "Or not."

"Thanks," Cole said.

"Just don't ignore what I said."

"Talk to you soon." Cole disconnected.

"Have you called Corwin yet?" Cole called out to Hanna.

"Not yet, you have her card. I was waiting 'til you got off the phone."

"No problem. I take care of it. I have more info for her."

Cole fished around his desk looking for California Corwin's card. He found a fist full of receipts, coupons, other people's cards, but no Cal Corwin.

"You're sure you don't have it?" Cole inquired.

A moment later Hanna was in the door, reaching for the phone. Stuck under the right corner of the phone was a card that read, 'California Investigations'.

"This it?"

Cole grinned sheepishly and said, "Good thing it wasn't a rattlesnake."

"Might have helped. Maybe you would have heard it rattle."

Hanna returned to her desk and Cole shrugged. He hated cards with two numbers. It meant you have a fifty-fifty chance of having to dial again. He decided on the cell number.

"Cal Corwin."

Bingo! Cole thought. "Ms. Corwin, Cole Sage."

"Well, hello. How am I so honored?"

"I have some information for you."

"Really?" Corwin truly sounded surprised.

"Your client, Mr. Chou. How well do you know him?"

"Not well. Like I told you, he was a referral," she replied.

"Here's what I got. He's Tong, deep Tong. He's got a kid who's in a street gang. Firecracker Boyz, You know them? FCBZ? They are the number one suspects in the New Year's Parade shootings. The kid has a miraculous way of getting out of drug, weapons, and assault charges without seeing the inside of a court room. These are dangerous people. Here's a theory. Somebody snatched her to get back at the brother. I'm thinking Norteños."

"Great. One problem with your theory. She packed a lunch. Took clothes."

"It doesn't take away from the fact that you are sniffing around some very private people who make people who get to close disappear."

"I appreciate your concern. But I've danced with some pretty scary partners. Besides, Mr. Chou is my client. Why would he hurt the one trying to find his daughter?"

"Oh, I don't know. Maybe she doesn't find said daughter." Cole was beginning to wish he hadn't called.

"Oh," Cal said flatly. "Thank you for the information, Mr. Sage, but I think we got off on the wrong foot. I was a cop for over ten years. I have been shot, cut, and had the shit beat out of me on numerous occasions. Don't let the scar on my face fool you. I was blown up. Get it? A bomb went off in my face. I'm still here and could kick your desk jockey ass in half a heartbeat. I appreciate your thinking you need to warn me about a few street punks and a bunch of old men. But really, I can take care of myself."

"I'm sorry. I missed the part after "thank you, Mr. Sage," Cole said brightly.

The line went dead.

"Hey, remind me I don't know that Corwin woman the next time she calls."

The phone on Cole's desk rang. "Sage."

"Too late," Hanna called through the door.

"Sorry," A voice said softly.

"Sorry, I didn't quite get that," Cole replied.

"I said 'I'm sorry'. You don't have to be an asshole about it." Cal Corwin's voice raised an octave.

"Apology accepted. You really do need to work on your people skills." Cole laughed.

"I know. I know." Cal laughed too. "One thing bothers me."

"What's that?"

"How come you know so much about the Chou family? What's your connection?"

Cole got up and closed his door.

"Sage? Sage! Are you there?" Cole heard Cal yelling as he picked the phone up.

"Yeah, I'm here. I had to close the door. Listen, I like you, you got a certain...."

"Irrefutable charm?" Cal interrupted.

"No, I was going to say 'chutzpah'," Cole chided. "Look, it seems we are on the same path, kind of, with completely different purposes. I'm going to let you in on something, but I need your word it goes no further."

"Done."

"Your client's son, Ricky, is an active participant in the kidnapping and imprisonment of my intern, Anthony Perez. I sent him to Chinatown to gather background for my story on the Parade shootings."

"When was that?" Cal asked.

"Three days ago."

"Why are you telling me this?"

"I might need your help? I have to tell somebody or my

head will explode? I just need someone to tell me it will be OK? To tell you the truth, I don't know."

"What do the police say?" Cal asked.

"They don't know."

"What? You haven't reported it? Why not?" Cal's voice increased in volume.

"The leader of the FCBZ, a stoner named Trick, was very clear in his demands. If they aren't met by tomorrow noon. They will, 'feed him to the sharks'. "

"What's he want?"

"Wants his cousin released from police custody. He's being held in connection with the Parade shooting," Cole said, as he tapped his pencil repeatedly on the desk.

"You want me to help get him back? Is that what this is?"

"It's being handled," Cole said coldly.

"Meaning?"

"The way they would do it."

"Hold on, Sage. You're no Bruce Willis. You don't know the first thing about dealing with gang warfare." Cal took a significant pause, then said, "Do you?"

"No. But Anthony has friends that do. They're here and have promised me they'll get him back."

"Let me tell you something, my friend, if this goes south, if someone is killed, you are an accessory and a co-conspirator in a gang related felony homicide. You will never see daylight again. If you live past your first gang confrontation in lock up. What the hell are you thinking?"

"I'm thinking Anthony is the closest thing I will ever have to a son. I would be right there with them if they would let me. I have no clue as to how and when and what they are about to do. I didn't ask for it, but I have complete deniability."

"Who are these people? Mission guys wouldn't be that dumb."

"They're from out of town. Anthony was no angel before I met him. He's gone to school, and is working on his Masters. He is completely out of that life. He doesn't know I called for help. He knows less than we do. We just know who has him."

"And how exactly is that?" Cal asked.

"I met with them. I met the top dog. I went looking for Anthony and stumbled into their path, probably the same way he did. These guys have that Tong connection, carries into the SFPD. They are like Teflon."

"What about your buddy, Lieutenant Chin? What's he say about all this?"

"I haven't told him."

"Shit, Sage, you are crazy. He is the only clean cop in Chinatown."

"That's why I didn't tell him. I don't want him dead, or disgraced, or God knows what."

"So, what do you want me to do?"

"I wanted you to know we are linked. I didn't want you blindsided with Chou family shrapnel."

Cole played with a paperclip with the tip of his pencil. For some reason, confiding in Cal Corwin lifted a heavy weight off of Cole's shoulders, chest really. He felt for the first time there was a plan. Luis and his guys, knew what to do. They would die trying, And that was more than anyone could ask.

"I will keep my ears open. I have a friend, employee kind of. Did you call your out of town friends on this line?"

"Yes."

"I'll have him scrub it. No more calls, Sage. None, zero, zip. Got it?"

"Got it."

"If there is anything you need, anything, call."

"I appreciate that but..."

"You told me. I either call the cops or become part of the plan. I don't have a lot of love for cops lately."

"Thank you, Cal."

"Not yet. Maybe never."

"No, for just giving me some clarity."

"I don't see how, but I'll take that."

"I'll be in touch," Cole said.

"I hope not," Cal chuckled. "Oh, and I really wouldn't kick your ass. I could but I don't think I will."

The line went dead.

"That's a comfort," Cole said to himself.

ELEVEN

"I'm tired of Tamales. They make my stomach hurt."

"How 'bout a granola bar?" Marco inquired.

"I want real food. I really want noodles. That would feel good to my stomach." Mei half groaned, half whined.

"I don't have any money," Marco apologized.

"I have some. My mama always gets me food that is soft in my stomach."

"Mei, we have to stay here. This is where we live now," Marco pleaded.

"I'm hungry for noodles." Mei was growing more and more upset. "We been up here forever. I want fresh air. I miss school. I want to go home." Mei began to cry.

"OK, we will go get some noodles. OK Mei, let's go get some noodles. We will buy you noodles. Then come right back. OK?" Marco was beginning to gently rock back and forth.

"Really?"

"We will go get noodles for Mei."

Mei moved quickly to her backpack. Unzipping the front pocket she removed a small Barbie wallet. She carefully took out a twenty dollar bill, tucked it back into the backpack, and zipped it up.

"Let's go!" Mei pushed her glasses up on her nose and flashed Marco an ear to ear smile. It was as if the noodle conversation never happened.

Out on the street, Marco and Mei looked up and down McClarren. This was a foreign land to the girl from Chinatown and the boy from south of Market. The early morning chaos of people rushing to work was gone. Few people were even to be seen. The pair walked several blocks in search of food before deciding to turn right on Clay Street.

"I'm hungry," Mei whined.

'I know, you said that back there. Do you see a place to eat?"

"I can't see very far Marco! You know that!"

"OK Mei. I will keep looking."

As they crossed an alley opening, Marco began to point excitedly. "That sign looks Chinese. Look at the sign Mei, look at the sign."

To Mei's delight, she could read the sign and she knew just what she would find inside. Hon's Wun Tun House smelled like home. Mei walked up to the first person she saw wearing a white shirt and black tie and asked in Cantonese if they served noodles. Receiving a positive response, she led Marco to the nearest table.

"I ordered us noodles!" Mei said excitedly.

"I like noodles." Marco nodded.

The two sat and rearranged the napkins, silverware,

and salt and soy sauce rack several times before the novelty wore off. The menus didn't matter to them, but they enjoyed looking at the pictures. Marco, not being familiar with Chinese restaurants and anything but take-out Chow Mein, giggled at the sight of the exotic dishes pictured in the menu. Mei patiently explained what they were and told him the Cantonese name for each. The time passed quickly, and before they knew it, the waiter brought two huge steaming bowls of noodles filled to the top with marvelous smelling broth.

"I got chicken! I don't like pork." Mei beamed.

"Smells good! Let's eat 'em up!' Marco closed his eyes, bowed his head, said something Mei couldn't hear, then made the sign of the cross and said, "Amen."

Across the room, sitting at a counter seat, sat a poorly dressed, greasy-haired man. Mickey Tucker, was a twenty-something. His obesity was bordering on the "morbidly" kind. Diners at the tables behind him found his smacking and grunting noises distasteful, to say the least. One couple actually moved to another booth. His dirty Cal Bears sweatshirt was splashed all down the front with a combination of General Taos Chicken and fried rice.

When he finally came up for a breath, Mickey saw Marco and Mei walking to their seats. Something was more important than his food, *them*. He didn't take his eyes off them for more than a minute. With his eyes glued to their every move, he reached, without looking, for his cell phone on the counter.

"Cal, Mickey."

"Hey Mick."

Mickey Tucker was California Corwin's computer-nerd-hacker-slacker. He worked with her on a part-time basis. Just enough hours and projects to buy new computer gear and allow him to be the go-to guy for gaming in San Francisco.

"You know that Chinese 'tard you were looking for?" he continued. "Tell me again what she looks like. Kinda fat? Pop bottle glasses? She with a Mexican lookin' retard?" He paused.

"That's not very nice. They have a disability, as do you, as I recall," Cal said.

"Is that a fat joke? I don't like fat jokes, Cal."

"It is not nice. Why are you asking?" Cal continued.

"Yeah, yeah I know it's not politically correct, I don't give a shit. They look like retards to me."

"What do you mean look like?" Cal said excitedly.

"I'm lookin' at them... I think."

"Where are you?"

"I'm having lunch, on Kearney, Hon's Wun Tun House. If it's them, they just came in."

"Do you think it's them?"

"Geez I don't know. How many Mexican Chinese Retard Combo Platters you think are in San Francisco?" Mickey choked, laughing at his own attempt to be funny.

"What's the number?"

"How the hell would I know?"

"Ask somebody!" Cal yelled into the phone.

Mickey got up and took a takeout menu from the rack at the end of the counter. "648, at Clay."

Cal lowered her voice and spoke slower, "Listen, Mickey. This is important. I want you to follow them. I'm on my way. Do not let them see you."

"They're re..." Mickey self-corrected. "They're *intellectually disabled*. You really think they're smart enough to notice me?"

"You can be seen from space, Mick. Yeah, they'll notice you."

"Enough with the fat jokes Cal, I mean it. I don't like fat jokes."

"Sorry, sorry. I'm on my way. Call me when you leave the restaurant."

"This'll cost ya."

Mei and Marco giggled, talked, and slurped their noodles. The long strands were warm and comforting. The broth felt good to Mei's stomach. Neither one noticed the fat, white guy staring at them from across the room.

When they finished, Mei gave Marco both fortune cookies. She paid the bill, left a dollar tip, and they left the restaurant. Mickey downed three diet Cokes with his double lunch and needed a bathroom break. Even though he did his business as fast as he could, his prey left the building before he came out. He tossed a twenty on the counter and said, "I'll be back for my change!"

In front of the restaurant, Mickey looked up and down both sides of the street. He was in a complete panic. A tall guy in a yellow plastic slicker passed Mickey singing *I Left My Heart in San Francisco* at the top of his voice. In front of the singer, was a shopping cart loaded with all his earthly possessions. As the cart rolled slowly down the handicap slope of the sidewalk at the corner, Mickey got a clear view of Marco and Mei about a hundred yards up the block.

Without thinking, Mickey broke into a dog trot in a valiant effort to catch the pair, moving farther and farther away from him. Mickey did pretty well the first twenty-five yards. His girth was not conducive to rapid movement. As he jogged along, between his panicked visions of Cal's reaction to his losing them, Mickey tried to figure out when the last time he ran was. He couldn't. At thirty yards, he was in a full sweat and breathing heavily. At forty yards, a sharp pain cut into his side, and at fifty yards, Mickey stopped. He would have put his hands on his knees and panted, but he couldn't reach them. A wave of nausea swept over him and a moment later two orders of General Taos Chicken and a double portion of fried rice blew into the gutter accompanied by three diet Cokes.

When he finished spitting, blowing his nose, and gasping, Mickey redirected his attention back to Mei and Marco. They were gone. He stood in the middle of the sidewalk with both hands on the top of his head. His eyes watered and his vision was blurred, but as far as he could see, there was no one on either side of the street.

"No, no, no, no no," Mickey repeated.

"Are you kiddin' me!" The voice he feared hearing the most, cut through the air. To his left, California Corwin stood next to her souped up Subaru Impreza.

"You lost them?" Cal yelled over the engine.

"I got sick," Mickey said sheepishly.

"*That* I can see! What I don't see is two kids you couldn't manage to follow!" Cal said, slamming the car door. Her engine screamed as she shot up the street.

For the next hour, Cal drove and walked a five block radius in front of where she left Mickey. Every person she passed was asked about the two kids. A picture of Mei was shown to anyone who would give her two seconds. A matted-haired man sat squatting against the wall of a marble front office building. From his posture he hadn't moved in quite a while.

"Have you seen two kids come by here in the last few minutes?" Cal asked.

"What kind of kids?" the man asked.

Cal was trying to be more sensitive, but before she realized she said, "Retarded."

"Got a couple bucks?"

"Do I look like a bank?" Cal snapped.

"Do I look like Wikipedia?"

Cal reached in her jeans pocket and pulled out several bills. No singles. She handed the guy a five dollar bill.

"They went down that alley about half hour a go."

"How do you know it was a half hour?" Cal grilled.

"The bus just went by a few minutes ago. I saw them when the bus before that came. The buses come every twenty minutes. So, I figure about a half hour." The man smiled up at Cal.

"You are looking more like Wikipedia all the time," Cal replied.

"And you look more like Wells Fargo!" the man said, putting his hand out.

"Don't press your luck," Cal said, stepping off the curb and heading for the alley.

The street sweeper had sprayed and brushed down the alley in just the last few minutes. The pavement was wet and the circular brush marks still showed where the sweeper rounded the corner. The alley was empty. The first solid lead was washed away, with Mickey's lack of physical fitness.

Cal walked the alley to the next street, and then the next. Nothing. But she had a neighborhood, a sighting, and an idea of where to focus. She walked back to the car and the homeless man.

"Here's the deal. If you see those kids again, you follow them and you see where they are hiding," Cal paused for dramatic effect. "It's fifty bucks for you. But I have to find them. Got it?"

"Hundred," The man said with another big cheesy grin.

"Like I said, don't press your luck."

"OK, OK, I'm in. How will you know when I find them?"

"You stay around here?"

"Not far."

"I will be around. A lot. Starting today. I'll check in with you often. Make yourself easy to find."

"For fifty bucks I'll stand naked in the middle of the street and wave my arms!"

"We'll save *that* celebration for later." Cal shook her head and grinned at the thought.

Luis and company were finding that being new in town definitely had its drawbacks. It took nearly forty-five minutes to find an abandoned building they felt comfortable breaking into. In the back of what must have been a liquor store or a Stop and Rob Market was a small two story building in the process of being renovated. Enough windows were damaged so as to almost be able to call it 'windowless'. Carlos jumped out of the front seat, bolt cutters in hand, and within seconds cut the chain on the security fence. The car was through the gate and the chain pulled through the chain link almost as quickly. Chuy pulled the car behind the first building.

"This is where you get out!" Luis said over his shoulder to Peter Lu.

Carlos jerked open the back door of the Corolla. Juan stepped out and reached back in and grabbed a handful of

Peter and his t-shirt, and pulled hard. Peter followed, once again hitting his head on the door jam.

The front door gave little resistance as Luis kicked the flimsy, makeshift plywood cover. Inside, the lack of windows made it easy to see around the construction site. In the center of the ground floor was a pile of plaster sacks. Next to them was a partial pallet of sheet rock. Luis gave his head a jerk, indicating the sheet rock.

Juan and Carlos roughly led Peter to the pallet and pushed him down on the stack.

"You seem like a reasonable guy. Probably good in math too." The other three laughed at Luis' stereotype joke. "Looks like you got good teeth, too."

"What do you what from me?" Peter said without looking at Luis.

"That's easy. We want our friend. I want you to tell me where he is. Easy, right?" Luis smiled but there was no humor or friendliness in it.

"I don't know what you're talking about."

"Ah, now homey, that's no way to be. I said it was easy. But you keep up that bad ass Chinaman routine and it becomes not so easy." Luis took his box cutter out of his hip pocket. "Now, where are they holding my friend?"

"You ain't shit compared to what Trick is. You think your little box cutter scares me? Shit, you ain't nothin' compared to what Trick can do!" Peter spit at Luis.

"Can he do this?" In a heartbeat Luis' vice-like grip clamped around Peter's throat. Luis slammed him backward onto the dusty flat surface of the sheet rock. "Now, one last time. Where is my hermano."

"Sek si!" Peter yelled.

Luis hit Peter hard in the face. A second later he was on

the stack of sheet rock, one knee firmly planted on each of Peter's arms. Peter kicked wildly and Luis hit him again in the jaw.

"We tried easy. Now we do it my way," Luis growled sliding open the shiny silver box cutter. With his left hand pinning Peter's neck to the sheetrock, his helpless captive's arms motionless, his eyes bulging, Luis moved quickly and with the precision of a surgeon. Moments later he'd carved a large XIV in Peter's forehead. Luis leaned back, loosened his grip a bit, and inspected his work.

"Go niang yang de!" Peter screamed.

"You think he's calling me names?" Luis asked Carlos.

"Sounds like."

Like a sculptor stepping back to examine his work, Luis tilted his head and squinted one eye. Then, without a word, he leaned down and made several deep cuts again. He swept the side of his hand across Peter's forehead. Little pink and red pieces of skin hit the sheet rock. The XIV was now carved an eighth of an inch wide and three inches tall in the Chinese boy's head.

Peter kicked and screamed profanities in Cantonese.

Luis slapped him hard across the face. "Pequeña perra! I'm getting tired of your sissy boy screaming, you little bitch! Shut the hell up."

Peter gasped as Luis' knee came up and slammed down in his stomach. Rolling and stepping down from the stack of sheet rock, Luis bent over and scooped up a handful of gypsum and dirt. He grabbed Peter's shoulder and rolled him and rubbed the handful of powder hard on the bloody open wound of his victim's forehead.

"Hard way," Luis said leaning over to where Peter lay. "Where is my friend? I can do harder. As a matter of fact,

I can do dead. It is your choice," Luis spoke softly and directly into Peter's face.

Peter didn't answer.

"I think this is a nice building. When do they work on it, do you think?" Luis asked, turning away from Peter.

Chuy looked around, "Not too often."

"I didn't think so either." Luis slapped Peter across the face. "Hey, you ever thought about one of those operations to fix your eyes to look more like us?" Luis tried to slap Peter again, but he threw his arms up blocking the blow.

"Quite the little fighter we got here!" Chuy laughed.

"I think he likes it here. I think we'll let him stay for a while. See if you can find some rope." Luis paused and looked down at the chalk white and blood red face below him. "I'll give you this, you think you're bad. I'm starting to get some of that San Francisco touchy feely shit. I think I won't kill you after all. Peace, brother." Luis laughed. "Hold his arms."

Juan and Chuy grabbed each of Peter's arms and forced him flat against the sheetrock.

"This is going to hurt like a son of a bitch. So, if you're even thinking about talking, I would hurry the hell up." Luis sighed at the silence. "I warned you."

On Peter's right arm was tattooed FCBZ and a Chinese symbol. In four quick deep cuts, Luis cut a box around the logo. Reaching out to Chuy palm open, his friend slapped a pocket utility tool across it. Struggling a bit to get it open, Luis soon opened and closed the needle nose pliers several times. After a couple of tries, Luis held enough skin in the grip of the tool to peel off the tattoo in one thick perfectly square piece.

"Tie him to that post over there." Luis tossed down the skin and wiped the blood off the pliers on Peter's t-shirt and handed them back to Chuy.

As Carlos and Juan dragged Peter over to a large supporting pillar, Luis cut a large rectangle of paper from a plaster sack. Without expression, he picked up the piece of tattooed skin and wrapped it in the paper.

An hour later, a manila envelope with TRICK written in fat, black felt tip pen, and a folded piece of plaster sack inside, was duct taped to a light pole in the center of Chinatown.

TWELVE

"I can't just sit here!"

"Sorry? I was on the phone," Hanna called from her desk.

"Nothing," Cole replied.

"That was a pretty loud nothing," Hanna said, moving to Cole's door.

"You're right. I've got to get out of here. The walls are closing in." Cole stood and left the office, heading for the elevator.

"Where are you going, Cole?"

"Counseling." The closing elevator doors nearly blocked Cole's reply.

Anthony's arms and wrists tingled as they drifted between numb and feeling. His keepers turned off the light on their last trip to slap him around. The earthy, iron taste of blood in his mouth was a constant reminder that he was in a situation he would probably not survive.

"'Irony'. Events that seem deliberately contrary to what one expects and are often amusing as a result," Anthony said into the darkness. "Well, Whisper, is this how it is going to go down? Four and a half years of college and the gangbangers have come back around to make sure you pay for your past sins? 'Irony', indeed."

He tried to twist and relieve pressure points in an effort to get some blood flowing to his arms and legs.

"Cole knows I'm missing. He's a smart guy. Don't worry. He's got this." Anthony believed every word, but as they were swallowed by the darkness, they felt hollow and unconvincing. "OK, so I'm Cole. What did I do? Call Lieutenant Chin? No, that's not Cole. I sniff around. Talk to people."

Anthony laughed. "He's probably in the basement, or on the next floor strapped to a chair! Now, that would be ironic."

He nervously sat clicking his front teeth together. Staring straight ahead, he saw his house in Los Angeles. His mother was on the porch wearing her favorite purple polka dot dress she loved so much. She died when Anthony was sixteen, but she looked healthy, happy, but most of all, alive. A lump came up in his throat.

"I will join you soon jefita. Tell the angels to get ready for me. I'm so sorry for the heartache I caused you." His mother blew him a kiss and disappeared in the darkness.

Throwing his head back, he sighed deeply, and tears rolled down his cheeks, "Now I'm talking to dead people. After all the scrapes I've been in, this one I walked into blind. This is one of Cole's stories, not mine. He's the one always getting knocked in the head or having the crap kicked out of him. I'm supposed to be an intern." The more he spoke, the madder Anthony got. Not at Cole, or the bunch down the hall, but at himself.

"I wish Heather was here." Anthony paused, then with an uncharacteristic burst of self-deprecation, said, "What kind of self-respecting vato has a thing for a girl named Heather?"

Heather Pollard is tall, blonde, and built like a swimmer. Anthony made sure, as a first year Journalism student that he always sat behind and to the side of her. As hard as he focused, took notes, and asked questions, he couldn't keep his eyes off her. Her way of framing a question was a thing of mystery to Anthony. He never felt limited in his language skills until he heard the beauty of her Connecticut eloquence.

It took two years, but he finally got the nerve to speak to her. They were assigned a project and had ended up in the same study group. The transition from street thug to serious college student was more mental than physical. Anthony's dress and grooming were more street than Ivy League.

It was Heather that got him to make so many changes.

"So, what's with the hair?" she asked at one of their late night study sessions.

"What?" Anthony responded.

The other members of the study group fell silent as the Connecticut beauty and the scary looking California Mexican stared at each other.

"You need a makeover. Corrine, don't you think he has possibilities?"

"Leave me out of this." Corrine giggled.

"What is this about?" Anthony asked, half angry with the backwards compliment.

"University of Chicago dress code. Gangbanger Chic is out this season. Journalist Cool is in."

"Where's that written?"

"In my note book. I'm a writer you know." Heather smiled and Anthony was smitten.

It was only a few days later she took him to a hair stylist salon filled with hot babes and gay guys. A petite beauty with ebony skin and a voice like Jamaican molasses sat Anthony in her chair and went to work as Heather sat watching.

When she spun the chair around, Anthony was shocked to see his hair was shorter than he ever remembered it, and parted. To his amazement he liked it.

"This too," Heather said, as she made circular motions with two fingers around her mouth and chin.

Within seconds, the clippers and electric razor trimmed and removed his sideburns, mustache, and goatee. Within an hour, Heather had him dressed in jeans that fit, a plaid oxford-cloth shirt, a woven hemp belt, and a forest green corduroy jacket. Within a month no one remembered what the reformed gangster looked like. But, Anthony re-membered. Heather had paid the bill for the makeover, he owed her, and wouldn't forget.

Their relationship was fire and ice. They laughed, teased, argued, and thoroughly enjoyed each other's company. It was apparent they would never be romantic. Her vibe, not his. As friends, comrades, and adversaries, though, they were a perfect match.

"My phone has GPS. They could find me with that!"

Anthony said brightly. "My worry is if they are the right ones looking.

The room down the hall had been silent for a long time. He wondered if there was anyone there.

"Maybe they got so toasted they forgot I was here."

Anthony closed his eyes and tried to come up with a strategy someone on the outside could be using to find him.

Cole closed his car door. He sat for a long moment in the early spring warmth of the solar heated interior. He looked down at the face of his daughter Erin on his cell phone and hit 'call'.

"Well, hello!"

"Second ring, that's pretty good," Cole said.

"It was your ringtone."

"Oh, and what might that be?"

"A Day in the Life," Erin replied proudly.

"The Beatles?"

"I read the news today, oh boy," Erin sang in a femme fatale John Lennon impersonation.

"Got a minute?" Cole asked.

"Uh, yeah, sure. What's up?"

"I don't want to interrupt anything."

"Are you alright, Dad? You sound funny," Erin said.

"Of course. Can't I call my favorite daughter without something being wrong?"

"I'm your only daughter. What's going on? You sound down."

"Alright, Dr. Mitchell, I need some counseling." Cole sarcastically teased.

"Hold on, I have to turn the heat down on the stove."

"Soup?"

"Spaghetti sauce. Ben and Jenny have become pasta fanatics." Cole heard the sound of a lid clang in the back ground. "So, what's going on?"

"Have you ever started something and half way through you wished you hadn't?" Cole began.

"You haven't taken up making stained glass!"

"No, no. Nothing like that," Cole chuckled. "No, I've done something kind of stupid."

"Remember Anthony Perez? The kid that I helped send to college? He's here in San Francisco and arranged to do his internship for his Masters with me at the paper."

"How wonderful," Erin interjected.

"Yeah, it was until three days ago. I sent him to gather background. I'm doing a piece on the Chinese New Year Shootings." Cole took a long uncomfortable pause. "He was grabbed by a street gang called The Fire Cracker Boyz. They want to swap him for a guy in jail."

"The police won't do that."

"They don't know."

"Anthony is kidnapped; you know it, and the police don't?"

"They have threatened to kill him if the guy isn't released from jail."

"And so?" Erin said firmly.

"And so, I called an old friend of Anthony's from L.A." Cole cleared his throat. "He is here and plans to get him back."

"Jenny! Be careful!"

Cole jerked the phone away from his ear.

"I'm sorry. Hold on a second," Erin said at a well-above-normal level. "Haven't I told you not to pour the big milk by yourself? Now look at the mess. I am right here. I would have poured it for you. You're just not big enough, OK?" Erin sounded stressed. "Oh no!" She screamed.

"Everything OK?" Cole asked.

"No, Jenny dumped a gallon of milk and my sauce just boiled over!"

"I'll call back, sounds like you're up to your neck," Cole interrupted.

"No, no, it's fine, really," Erin said unconvincingly.

"I'll catch you later, sweetheart. Hugs to Jenny." Cole clicked off the phone before Erin could answer. She didn't call back.

Cole got out of the car and started down the street.

"Who did this?" Trick screamed. "Who disrespected us this way, our street, our community?"

Trick paced the living room like a caged animal. Not a word was said by the FCBZ crew in the room. Some were hardly breathing. They knew when Trick was in such a blind rage anything was possible, and probable. A kind of madness over took him. He was inconsolable. It was better to leave him alone. Let him scream.

No one went for the door, they all looked at it, they all wanted to leave, but no one dared. You very likely would get a bullet in the back.

"If they think we will take this..." Trick's thoughts drifted as he went to the window. "Right under our noses! Why didn't one of you see this?" He turned and looked at each face in the room. "He thrust his hand, open palm, toward the window, "Right under our noses!" His screaming was beginning to bring a hoarseness to his voice.

"Tomorrow! Tomorrow they will wish they were never born! We will hit them with everything we got. Every bullet will be spent filling their rat hole neighborhood with blood." Trick was panting from the force of his screaming.

Anthony listened from down the hall. He recognized out of control. Trick was two notches up the dial from totally gone. The rage he heard could bring anything. He feared the end was near. Maybe their strike out at the Norteños will get them all killed. Anthony gave a sad grin in the darkness at his wishful thinking.

The reality was, he had no idea what kind of offense could light such burning rage in Trick. What had they done to him? Was it one of his crew? It has to be a massive insult. No successful retaliation could possibly come from such rage. Someone will be killed, or arrested. Anthony just hoped the former wouldn't be him.

As Trick ranted, and Anthony worried, Chuy stood in a shady, obscured spot across the street. He was dressed in a green and gold Oakland A's sweatshirt and a pair of khaki walking shorts. His hair was pulled back in a short pony tail and covered with a green A's beany. Chuy patiently stood, unnoticed, casually watching the tourists and the third story window of the building across the street.

As Cole drove across the Golden Gate Bridge, off to the west, fog was beginning to burn off. To his right, the city was awash in sunshine and the white caps on the bay sparkled. He meant to call Kelly. He wanted to call Kelly. Somehow it just didn't feel right. As he headed north to Sausalito, his thoughts were on her smile and the welcoming hug he would receive at her door.

The tide was out and the houseboats of Sausalito's Richardson Bay sat low in their moorings. Some rested in the mud, and looked sad and abandoned. In an hour or so they would begin to ride high again and take on the charm and grace of their middle to high six-figure price tag.

It felt strange to Cole to walk down the gangplank. The houseboat was a good three feet lower than normal. Then he realized he'd never been to Kelly's at low tide. He hoped it wasn't a harbinger of bad tidings.

For a long moment Cole stood staring at the pattern on the front door. Before he could knock, he heard foot steps behind him.

"Hey, what are you doing here in the middle of the day?"

"Hi, I was just..."

"Not passing by?" Kelly said sarcastically.

"No. I needed to see you."

"Anything wrong?"

"Does something have to be wrong for me to want to see you?"

"There is if you show up without warning." Kelly reached Cole and put her hand on the side of his arm. "Let's go in."

Cole followed as Kelly unlocked the door and went in. He shrugged his shoulders at her back. No hug for me, he thought.

He closed the door behind him and, as he turned, Kelly put her arms around his neck and pressed her cheek against his.

"What's a matter, sweetheart?" She whispered.

"I need you to be the pin that the needle of my moral compass rests on."

Kelly stepped back from their embrace. She tilted her head and squinted slightly. "What's going on Cole?"

"I was so sure about my decision to call Luis and the guys from LA. Now I'm not. I'm really torn. I'm supposed to be the fighter for good, justice, equality, and all the things that separate us from the bad guys. Not join up the first time my back is against the wall." Cole crossed the room and sat down hard in a chair next to the window. "On the other hand, I would be right there with them, if they'd have let me. Fighting to get Anthony out of danger. It's driving me nuts."

"'To the pure, all things are pure, but to those who are corrupted and do not believe, nothing is pure. In fact, both their minds and consciences are corrupted.' Titus 1:15." Kelly read from an open Bible on the counter. "I found that last night."

"So, what's that make me?"

"Torn. You know what's right. You know what's wrong. Kind of like oil and vinegar. They don't mix well."

Out the window, a small skiff glided across the shallows. Kelly moved across the room to the chair across from Cole. They sat quietly looking out at the rising tide.

Several minutes passed. Cole spoke without looking at Kelly, "What would you have done?"

"You have been so many places, seen so many things that I can't begin to imagine. Your values and perceptions are based on a life lived as a first hand observer of how terrible mankind can be. So, I have no idea what I would have done. I can assure you of this, if anything but the path you've taken would get Anthony killed, then I surely would have gotten him killed."

"How can you be with someone like me then?"

"With you I feel safe. Not just physically, but emotionally as well. Since I've known you, I have seen such growth in you spiritually and emotionally. You have shown me that your heart is where it should be. Are you perfect? Heaven's no. But are you working on becoming a comforter to me and a man God is proud to call his own? Yes, I see it more every day.

"I don't think you know how much you mean to me, to Erin, even Ben has such an admiration for you." A shifting of the houseboat and a loud creak gave her pause. "So, if you're struggling with this decision, it's no wonder. The thing that sets you apart from most people is that it is a struggle. Our human nature says, let's go get him! Kill the bad guys! Our better nature says, there must be a better way. It's our knowledge of God's love that causes the struggle. There is a verse, in Romans I think, that says "Do not pay anyone back evil for evil, but focus your thoughts on what is right."

"We should get you a radio or TV show. You're quite a preacher." Cole smiled.

"It not preaching. It's love. It hurts me to see you so conflicted. It is my faith that has taught me that our ways aren't God's ways. I struggle too. I'm not being holier than thou." Kelly sounded hurt.

"That was a compliment. It didn't come out quite right," Cole offered.

Kelly got up and sat across Cole's lap, rested her head on his shoulder and put her arm around his neck. "How long can I hold you?

"I need to be back by four."

They sat silent for a long while. The house boat continued to shift and groan as the water level continued to rise. Kelly gently stroked Cole's cheek.

"The worst will be over soon," Cole said breaking the silence.

"I hope so," Kelly said, then kissed him softly.

As was his habit, Trick surrendered his rage to large amounts of weed and beer. His manic rage was self-medicated to the point of near unconsciousness. This, of course, was seen as license for the rest of the Fire Cracker Boyz to follow suit. Soon the insane screaming gave way to the heavy bass thump of thug-life hip hop and rap music.

Beer runs were frequent and bags of Blue Velvet marijuana buds were brought from their hiding place to be opened and scattered on the table. The afternoon passed with no further outbursts. Around four o'clock, Trick stumbled to the couch in a smoky daze. Two guys on the couch moved quickly to get out of the way as Trick flopped down facing the back of the couch.

No one in the front room gave a thought to the young man down the hall duct taped to a chair. Anthony closed his eyes in complete exhaustion a while after the music started. He fell into a deep hard sleep.

The Fire Cracker crew played mahjong, sent text messages, sipped beer, smoked large quantities of bud, and wasted away the afternoon. The steady beat of the boom box lulled the third floor into a false sense of safety.

THIRTEEN

At three-thirty, Carlos, dressed in Giant's orange and black from head to foot, took Chuy's spot across from the FCBZ hangout. The alcove proved to be a perfect location to observe and not be noticed. The entry was so narrow that most people walked past without even seeing it. Chuy only moved aside for one old bent lady in the three hours he stood watch. He helped her open the door and get her small aluminum frame shopping cart through the door. Once through the door, she reached into a Knob Hill grocery bag and pulled out a cookie. She smiled and handed it to Chuy and went on her way.

"Luis says we move at five," Carlos said, as he slipped in the narrow space. "It will be almost dark by then. Has that space turned over?" he pointed at a white Honda parked in front of the building across the street.

"Yeah, bunch of times."

"I'm supposed to discourage anyone from being there at five."

"I'll be back in a second. I saw something that might help."

Five minutes later Chuy returned carrying three orange and yellow AT&T traffic cones.

"How's that?" Chuy said with a broad grin.

"Oughta do it." Carlos nodded.

The two old friends fist-bumped and Chuy slipped into the crowd jamming the sidewalk.

As the afternoon sun began to fade, so did the crowds. The white Honda was replaced three or four times, but at about a quarter to five, when a silver Lexus pulled away, Carlos casually made his way across the street and placed the traffic cones in the space. No one noticed.

He positioned himself in front of the restaurant just south of the building he watched so diligently. Three times FCBZs left the building, one came back with a grocery bag, one with a twelve pack of Keystone, and the third guy hadn't returned. None of them bothered to look up or down the block. Carlos went unnoticed.

At five o'clock on the dot, the old green Corolla rolled up the street. Carlos removed the cones and Chuy parked. No one got out, but Carlos climbed into the back seat.

"See anything?" Luis inquired.

"Nothing really. Lot of people buying crap for their next garage sale."

"We'll just sit here until it gets a bit darker. Juan, let me see your phone."

Luis put in a number from memory. "Sage? Are you at work? We will come see you in the next hour. I'll call you when we leave." Luis handed the phone back to Juan. "I don't know how to turn it off."

"Red button."

The four men sat in silence. Chuy closed his eyes and leaned his head back. Carlos and Juan looked out the windows and watched the lights start to come on along the street. Luis stared straight ahead, motionless.

The few people on the street seemed to be either looking for a place to eat or heading for their car. A very stiff man in a long sleeve shirt and navy blue tie turned off the lights and locked the door of the jade jewelry shop on the ground floor of the building. The Corolla sat in darkness.

It was nearly six o'clock when Luis jerked his head from side to side, popping his neck. He stretched his arms out in front of him and groaned.

"Let's get this thing done. Chuy, you open the trunk. Listen, I don't want anybody dead on purpose. Beat the shit out of them. Knock their heads off, but don't kill 'em, you got me? If we step in it worse than we think, they start shooting, Juan, Carlos let 'em have it. I prefer knees. If you got to take 'em out, well," Luis shrugged. "You make the call. We got the surprise thing on our side. Hit 'em, hit 'em real hard. Let's hope we break something and they don't get up. Once inside, I'll find Whisper."

A young couple, wearing matching *Carmel by the Sea* sweatshirts pushing a stroller, leisurely passed by the car.

"OK," Luis said calmly.

Chuy crossed himself and got out of the car. Once out of the car, Luis moved to the building's upstairs entrance. Juan and Carlos each took a baseball bat from the trunk of the car. They all moved quickly, quietly, and with purpose.

Luis tried the door and it was locked. Chuy stepped forward and took a small black crow bar from his waist band. He slipped it into the door casing just behind the battered doorknob. With a combination of a quick jerk and a shove of his shoulder the door popped open. He turned and grinned at the others. They moved inside and closed the door behind them.

Luis moved quietly up four or five steps. The men stood and listened for movement upstairs. Luis pointed at the light fixture overhead and gave an across-the-throat cutting movement with the side of his hand. Carlos glanced around and, finding the light switch, cast the stairs into partial darkness.

As the group approached the first landing, the sound of a door closing came from one of the floors above. The four men pressed against the wall. Rapid footsteps descended the stairs. Strobe-like shadows flashed across the second floor landing and down the stairwell. Luis reached over to where Chuy stood and took his baseball bat.

The footsteps reached the second floor landing. The wall sconce cast an amber tinted light on the face of a young Chinese runner wearing an FCBZ cap and a white t-shirt. Without stopping he continued his rapid decent. On the first floor landing, the young man stopped for a couple seconds and felt the wall for a light switch. Not finding one, he continued to the ground floor. A regrettable decision.

He was nearly on top of Luis before he sensed his presence. It was too late. In one fast, brutal movement Luis spun the runner around. One sinewy hand on each end of the bat, Luis pushed it cross the runner's throat, cutting off his air and slamming his head hard against the wall, knocking off his FCBZ cap.

Luis leaned in within inches of his captive's ear, "Where is the one you guys are holding?"

A hoarse garble of profanity came from the Asian's

mouth. Luis shoved his thumb inside the runner's mouth and pulled his cheek hard to the left, his head followed. Luis brought the bat down hard on his collar bone, a stomach-turning crack filled the darkened stair well. In an instant the bat pinned the groaning runner back against the wall. Luis whispered once again, "The next one will crush your skull. Where is my friend kept?"

"Back room. Down the hall," The runner gasped.

"Thank you," Luis said softly pulling the bat from the young man's throat.

The runner grabbed his throat and doubled over. Luis came down hard on the back of his head. He went limp. Chuy rolled him down the stairs with the tip of his heavy steel-toed work boot. Carlos pushed the motionless body tightly against the door.

"Remember he's there on the way out," Juan said quietly.

The first floor was lit only by a sconce on the landing and a small fixture on the celling half way up the hallway. All the doors that were visible bore the names of businesses painted in English and Chinese. The second floor appeared to be empty. Most of the doors stood open. Empty boxes and trash cluttered the hallway.

The third floor landing benefited from a shaft of light coming off the back of a hotel sign through the window at the end of the hall. There were only four doors on this floor. From watching the windows from below, the crew from L.A. knew the apartment they were looking for was the first door on the left.

The thump, thump, thump of Hip Hop seemed to move the peeling chocolate brown door in and out like the cone on a speaker. Chuy stood on the right side of the door. Luis on the left. Carlos and Juan stood to the side. As he moved to the center of the door, Luis turned, and in an uncharacteristic moment of affection, winked at Carlos.

Luis nodded at Chuy, and handed him back his bat, then took a step backwards. Then, with an incredibly forceful blow, kicked the door wide open.

"Joder a los bastardos!" Luis screamed as the four men rushed through the door.

Chuy swung hard and hit the first guy he came to across the jaw with the bat. He went down. Two FCBZ were still sitting at the table, blunts in hand, as Juan hit one across the top of his arm crushing his humerus. His friend watched in stoned disbelief as Juan drove the bat through his shoulder joint. Both men collapsed on the floor screaming.

A shiny, chrome box cutter slashed three deep cuts across a white t-shirt as Luis nearly eviscerated the first FCBZ in his line of sight. The shirt turned to scarlet as its owner just stood, mouth agape, looking down in horror.

The pock-marked thug that Cole encountered on his trip into Chinatown stood with his back to the window. In what seemed like slow motion, he pulled a 9mm automatic from his waist band and racked a round into the chamber as Carlos watched from just inside the door.

"Gun!" Carlos yelled, dropping his bat and pulling his own gun.

Pockmark looked Carlos right in the eyes as he raised his gun to fire. Carlos stood calm and unwavering as he recalled Luis' order not to kill. He smiled at Pockmark and fired twice, hitting him once in the knee and once in the opposite thigh. Pockmark dropped his gun and collapsed on the floor.

Ricky Chou, in a moment of panic, dove under the table. In complete terror, he watched between the legs of a chair as his comrades fell one by one. His hands trembled as pulled his handgun from his waistband and held it for a long moment. His mind raced, he knew he must do something, but he was paralyzed in fear. He did not want to die.

Trick Zhuó had been dozing on the couch when the door exploded inward. He was still shaking his head and blinking his eyes, trying his best of clear the cobwebs. As he stood, drugs and alcohol still swirling through is system, he found it difficult to steady himself.

Luis turned and rushed down the hall. At the far end was a door. Without breaking stride he hit the door shattering the casing and breaking the two top hinges. As the door dangled by one twisted bottom hinge, light flooded the darkened room. Luis saw his old friend. He knew it was Whisper, by his eyes, but so much else had changed that he hardly knew him.

"You're a long way from home Ese." Anthony smiled.

"Only because I have to save your sorry ass."

Luis moved quickly and used his box cutter to free Anthony from the duct tape binds holding him to the chair. He took his friend by the arm and tried to help him stand.

"Can you walk?"

"I think so," Anthony replied.

"You hurt?'

"Huh uh, they just slapped me around a bit.

With that, Luis threw his arms around his friend and gave Anthony a bear hug. "Damn, you scared the shit out of me. How'd you get in this mess?" he said, as he let go.

"They saw my tat," He said, holding out his hand.

"We gotta get you outta here." Luis moved for the open door.

Anthony rubbed his wrist and jumped up and down several times trying to get his circulation and muscles back on line.

As Luis entered the living room, he stomped the plug in the wall to the right of the door and the music stopped.

Carlos and Juan both stood, guns drawn, and pointed at the three FCBZ still able to stand. The guy Luis had slashed was slumped against the wall holding his stomach and crying. Movement in the room stopped, but not Trick's mouth.

"I will track you down and I will kill all of you. You have disrespected my crew, my neighborhood, and the Chinese people!" Trick screamed. All pretense of the cool gangster chief was gone. He was out of his mind with anger.

Ricky Chou watched breathlessly from under the table as Luis and Anthony entered the room. The heavy mahogany chair's thick back and legs hid his crouched form. His shoulder pressed him hard against the floor, his gun rested on the cross bar between the chair's back legs. This was his last chance to act. He aimed carefully between the vertical maze of wooden legs at Anthony's chest.

Ricky glanced around the room. His friends and comrades lie everywhere, unconscious, bleeding, groaning and he was hiding behind a chair. His shame and cowardice clung to him like a spider webs. This was his chance to redeem himself. He must fire. He would shoot the newspaper guy and then their leader. He would be a hero and Trick would see his real value at last. If Trick would just stop screaming!

Ricky slowly pulled the trigger, it felt thick and heavy. He closed his eyes and fired. The report of the 9 mm was thunderous. He opened his eyes to take aim at Luis. In front of him stood Trick, a large, crimson spot growing larger and larger on the back of his snow white t-shirt.

"Let's go!" Luis shouted as he turned toward the door. "Come on!" he grabbed Anthony by the arm and pulled him toward the door.

Ricky stood and watched as Trick fell in a twisted, contorted heap, face down on the carpet. Chuy followed Luis out the door, with Carlos close behind. As Juan turned for the door, Ricky raised his gun and fired again, hitting Juan's left upper arm. Juan spun and fired as he backed out the door, missing Ricky with both shots.

The apartment was still. The manic three minutes of violence was over. The only sound was the groaning and whimpering of the wounded. Ricky ran to where Trick lay motionless.

"Trick!" Ricky called as he rolled his friend over. Trick Zhuó stared at the ceiling, his face without expression. A large red stain on his chest left no doubt he was dead. Ricky shook Trick's shoulders and cried.

It was nearly fifteen minutes later when Ricky stood up. As he took in the carnage in the apartment, his eyes caught a familiar reflection in the window behind the table. His t-shirt was still white. His arms were straight. His face looked just like always. He wasn't shot or beaten, he had no broken bones. He wasn't harmed in any way.

Yet, three broken bodies lay where they fell. Calvin Tao passed out from loss of blood. The wounds were still seeping from the slashes inflicted by Luis. He leaned against the wall, his chin on his chest. There were groans coming from the side of the table near the window, but Ricky couldn't look.

His gun lay on the floor next to Trick. By rights, Ricky

was now the leader of the Fire Cracker Boys. He had to get away. He couldn't stand the smell of the stale marijuana smoke and spilled beer in the apartment. The sounds of his injured friends roared in his head.

"I will make them pay," Ricky said to no one. "They will pay for this." He reached down and picked up his gun.

Gun in hand, he ran from the apartment. He didn't stop running until he reached his car. The chirp-chirp of the alarm seemed to bounce from every wall along the street. One old bent man pushed a walker with the evening shopping on the seat in a small yellow bag. Ricky got in his car and pulled onto the empty street.

The Corolla was winding its way toward the Chronicle Building. Juan's wound was wrapped tight in a torn towel Chuy found in the trunk. Not the most sanitary dressing, but it appeared to be relatively clean. Juan was sure the bullet hadn't hit bone, but there were holes on both sides of his arm.

The back seat was a bit crowded but no one seemed to mind.

"Sage, Luis. Somebody wants to talk to you."

"Cole?" Anthony said, sounding more hoarse than usual.

"Oh, thank God! Are you OK, buddy?" Cole felt tears well up.

"I'm good. I'm good." Tears streamed down Anthony's cheeks with the realization he was going to be alright. He handed the phone back to Luis.

"Sage, we got a problem, man. Juan took a bullet. He's not dyin' or nothin'. He got shot in the arm. He needs sewed up pretty bad." Luis paused. "Know anybody?"

"Yeah, where are you?"

"About five or ten minutes from you."

"I'll make a call. See you out front."

"Good."

Cole picked up the land line and hit speed dial button number one.

"Erin, I need some help. Is Ben home?"

"No, what's the matter."

"Will he be home soon?"

"No, he's taking another doctor's shift tonight. Dad, you're scaring me. Are you OK?"

"Yeah, sweetie I'm fine. But, a friend of mine needs a look at. Do you have a medical kit?"

"Of course. What's going on?"

"If I tell you, you could get in trouble. So let's just say he had an accident and doesn't have Obamacare yet."

"And so..."

"So, I'll see you in a half hour, I hope."

Cole grabbed his jacket and ran to get his car from the garage. Five minutes later he was parked illegally at the curb in front of the Chronicle. Two minutes after that, the Corolla pulled up behind.

Anthony got out and approached Cole's car. Cole spotted them in the side mirror and jumped out.

"I'm sorry, Cole," were Anthony's first words.

"Nothing to be sorry for," Cole replied. "Hell of a way to get a story, though."

The two men high-fived and laughed with relief.

"You take school boy and we'll follow," Luis said and the Corolla pulled up to Cole's car.

Traffic was light and the trip to Erin's took a little less than thirty minutes. Cole and Anthony mostly sat in silence on the way. Cole didn't want to just fill the air with idle chatter. The two men shared a bond, but it was one of mutual respect. Cole hadn't given Anthony a hug because it just was out of character.

Anthony wanted to say something. The problem was he couldn't find the words. He felt like a deep sea diver who had risen to the surface too quickly. So many sounds and visions flashed through his mind as he looked out into the night. He was alive. His old life was swirling together with his new life. He felt afraid. The old life rose to save the new. His new life was like a new-born colt trying to steady itself for the first time on fragile, shaking legs. As car lights shone into the windows, he wondered who he really was. Anthony had become so completely submerged into the world of college, writing, and people the likes of which he had never known. His old life seemed long ago and far away. As they moved through the dark, Anthony let his old life slip into the dark San Francisco night.

Erin stood in the opened door as Cole pulled into the far side of the driveway. Chuy backed in the Corolla next to Cole. As the men moved toward the door, Anthony stayed several steps behind.

"Hi, Sweetie," Cole said approaching the door.

Father and daughter gave each other a quick embrace. The group behind Cole stood quietly as he made the introductions and Erin welcomed them into her home. Anthony stood back and waited for his friends to go inside. He approached the porch and gave Erin a sheepish smile.

"So this is my adopted bother, huh?"

"That is an honor I am unworthy of," Anthony said, a bit taken aback by Erin's remark.

Erin stepped down from the porch and gave Anthony a hug. "My dad thinks the world of you. You must be pretty special," She said softly.

"Thank you. And thank you for helping my friend."

"What have we got here?" Erin asked Cole.

"Juan seems to have a hole in his arm. Have you ever stitched anybody up?"

"A gunshot wound? Dad, that must be reported."

"I said 'a hole'. Nothing about a gunshot wound. This is neither a hospital nor a doctor's office and there is no doctor around that I can see. So, I don't think a private home qualifies for a report agency, if in fact there were a gunshot wound, which, as I said, no one has mentioned except you."

"He could sell snowballs to Eskimos!" Erin said, shaking her head. "Let's go see what we have here."

"She's got your temper." Anthony laughed.

"I don't have a temper," Cole said to himself.

Luis had led the group to the kitchen. Juan sat at the kitchen table and the others stood in front of the sliding glass door leading to the patio. As Erin came into the room, Luis stepped forward and gave her a nod and half bow of respect.

"We are grateful for your help. We are strangers around here and your father was kind enough to offer help."

"I'm Erin and my dad has never met a rule he wasn't willing to bend a bit." She extended her hand to Luis and then to Carlos and Chuy. "So, you must be the one with the owie."

"Yeah, kinda," Juan offered.

"I usually work with children. I didn't mean to make fun of your injury."

"That's cool. I just figure it ran in your family." Juan turned and grinned at Cole.

"I didn't tell you they are all part of a traveling comedy troupe," Cole said.

Erin gently unwrapped the dirty orange towel from Juan's arm. "This is pretty grungy but it seems to have done the trick. There is no significant bleeding."

The kitchen table was covered in a pale green cloth. There were several sterile dressing packs lying on the table. Two plastic bottles, one clear and one green, were at the ready, as were packs of sterile suture strips and butterfly tape stitches. Erin was prepared, calm, and in control.

"So, the unidentified flying object entered here and exited here. A nice clean wound. I'm going to flush it out with an antibacterial rinse. It will have a cool, tingly effect. Then I'm going to give you three or four stiches on the exit side of the wound. The entry point I will dress and leave open to allow draining. If any puss or strange, colored fluid is visible when you change the dressing in a couple of days, run, don't walk, to the nearest hospital. That is, unless you want to lose that nicely illustrated arm of yours. Got it?"

"Yes, ma'am," Juan said softly.

"Let's get started." Erin smiled and patted Juan's hand reassuringly.

She picked up the green bottle printed with a long medical name. She inserted the pointed tip of the bottle about an inch into the wound. Juan's eye's involuntarily winced closed.

"You OK?"

Juan nodded.

A slightly foamy, burgundy fluid ran from the exit point of the wound. Erin gently squeezed the bottle again and a pinkish fluid drained from the wound.

"That look's good," Erin said. "Ok, this is going to hurt a bit. Erin tore open the pack with a sterile needle and fine black thread.

"It hurts already, I *problee* won't notice." Juan gave a nervous chuckle.

Erin's experience and confidence was evident as she worked quickly and professionally, closing up the quarter-sized hole in Juan's arm. The entire procedure took about five minutes. Juan was stitched, packed, and bandaged.

"This is used, but clean," Erin said, as she fitted Juan with a navy blue sling. "Take a couple of these every six hours and you should be OK. Don't forget, any yellow or white fluid from your wound, straight to the hospital. Got it?"

"Yes. Thank you for your help. What do I owe you?"

"My dad's got this one."

Juan stood and looked at Luis and the others.

"Time for us to go home," Luis said, moving toward Erin. "Your old man is a pretty righteous guy. He did a good job on you, too," Luis nodded and gave Erin a smile. "Thank you for your help. We appreciate it. Take care of these two. I have a feeling they are going to get into a lot of trouble." Luis jerked his head toward where Cole and Anthony stood.

As Cole stayed behind, the five old friends made their way to the front door. Chuy went to the car and started the engine. Carlos got the rear door for Juan and went around the car and got in.

Anthony and Luis stood on the lawn half way to the car.

"This is the last time I save your ass, hermano. We live in different worlds now. You will always be my homeboy, but that will fade away too. If you listen to the old man, you'll end up a famous writer. You were always too smart to be stuck in the barrio anyways."

"Luis, I..."

"We're cool. No need for words," Luis interrupted.

The two embraced and they parted. Luis tasseled Anthony's strange, new haircut.

"Stay out of trouble, homie," Luis said, turning for the car.

"Whisper" was dead. Anthony Perez was free to be a new person. Free of the past, the cord cut, all debts paid. As he watched the tail lights disappear up the street, he felt oddly relieved. There was no sadness or remorse, just a weight lifted. There was nothing to go back to.

Erin and Cole stood on the porch looking at Anthony's back.

"We need to have a talk."

"Where's Jenny?"

"Next door having pizza and a movie with Karina. Don't change the subject."

"Anthony there was kidnapped by a gang of Chinese thugs called the Fire Cracker Boyz. I sent him on the assignment that put him in their way. Luis and the boys came to get him back. Juan got hurt in the process. The best daughter in the world fixed him up without questions. And he just said good-bye to his past and embraced his future. I'm proud of him. And I love *you* very much. That's 'bout it."

"No police?"

"Street justice."

"You have a very strange sense of justice."

"Sometimes the rules need to be adjusted to fit the game."

"It's the game I worry about. Or, how many seasons you're going to be able to play."

"I'm not sure, but I think I'm looking at my replacement," Cole said, putting his arm around Erin's shoulder.

FOURTEEN

Cal shoved the last bite of bagel and pineapple cream cheese into the little brown sack on the passenger seat. Her mind was a distracted jumble of her plan for the day, the conversation with Mr. Chou the night before, and his demands for the immediate return of his daughter. Her assurances that she was closing in were of little consequence. The threats of payment refusal, and not-so-veiled threats of her disappearance if anything happened to Mei, left Cal with indigestion and a fitful night's sleep.

At straight up eight o'clock, Cal turned the corner onto McClarren. The sidewalks were still crowded, and the street was bumper to bumper with cars waiting to get into parking garages. Cal repeatedly pushed the radio pre-set radio stations. All the pre-sets were news and news talk radio stations. The nervous habit was acquired years ago when she used to jump from station to station looking for a song she liked. She rarely landed on a news story she listened to, so the station jumping continued.

A bumper sticker in front of her that spelled out "coexist" held Cal's attention as she tried to identify the various religious symbols making up the word. Muslim crescent and star, peace sign, Om symbol in Devanagari script; Cal was quite proud she knew the name of that one. The Star of David came next, but she was stuck on the "i". The dot on the "i" was a ships wheel. As she pondered the possible meanings and tried to determine the religions it could possibly represent, Cal was startled by a knock at her window.

"Hey, Wells Fargo!"

It was the homeless guy Cal called 'Wiki'. She had recruited him to keep an eye out for the kids.

Cal rolled down her window and leaned back from the grizzly face and malodorous breath in her window. "Wiki, what's up?"

"I found them. I know where and how. Gonna cost a bit more for the keys to the kingdom." The matted beard and moustache parted as he opened wide for a grin that exposed rotted, snaggled, and broken teeth.

"First I get them."

"What you gonna do with a couple of mongoloid children? You one sick lady." The man's vile breath made Cal wince and pull back involuntarily.

"I'm a P.I. and I am finding them for the family. Nothing sick about that," Cal reprimanded.

"Whatever you say." The Wiki giggled. "I'm jist concerned about Mr. Franklin taken a nice nap in my pocket."

"Mei first, money later."

"OK, OK. Pull into the alley here," he indicated an alley on her right three car lengths ahead. "I'll show you where you wanna go."

It took several minutes, but Cal found herself in the alley next to 415. She pulled up tight against the wall and got out. The homeless man stood quite proud of himself in front of a steel door. Cal realized she had been down this alley and had even tried the door. What's he trying to pull, she thought.

"It's locked," Cal said sarcastically.

"That's why I am so valuable, Miss Fargo." Wiki laughed at his joke.

"Alright. I give. What's the catch?"

"I know where the key is and you don't! Catch of the day, huh?"

"You can get me in without blowing a hole in the wall or knocking the door down? I want the kids, but not enough to comment burglary." Cal knew she had him.

"So, I get a Franklin?"

"I guess you do. If I come out that door with the two kids."

"We got a deal?"

"Yes. We have a deal."

"Then leave General Grant here to keep me company." Wiki's voice grew dark and ominous.

"No can do," Cal said, reaching in her pocket and pulling out a money clip. "How about the Jackson twins and Mr. Hamilton?"

"Michael and Latoya?" Wiki burst into laughter. Cal grinned to see someone enjoy himself so much.

Cal handed Wiki the three bills. He turned and moved quickly to the electrical boxes on the wall. He popped open the box where the key hung and nearly glided to the door. Wiki unlocked the door and disappeared into the dimly lit room. A few moments later, another door opened casting a wide beam of light into the room. Cal followed and, as she entered the lobby area, saw Wiki standing at an elevator.

"I followed them to the elevator. The numbers above the door said 14. That's as far as I went. Figured that would do. It'll do, right?"

"You are a regular Sherlock Holmes, Mr. Wiki." Cal smiled.

Wiki hit the down button, turned without a word and headed back outside. Cal glanced around the lobby. The sound of the cables and their mechanism echoed through the empty building as the elevator reached the lobby.

Cal looked at herself in the shiny elevator walls. She turned her head slightly and looked at the scar along her jaw and neck. The door opened, the brass plaque across the hall read '14th Floor'.

The hallway must have run a hundred feet in each direction. Cal stood silent, eyes closed for a long moment. Silence, in all directions. She moved forward, pausing briefly at each door. "Don't rush," she said softly, "no hurry." As she reached the windows at the end of the hall, Cal leaned against the rail. She knew she would find them, but her heart raced. She felt like a dog that chases cars, never giving a thought to what he would do if he caught one. She was minutes from finding two kids who are mentally impaired. How would they react? What if they were non-compliant? What then? Cal sighed deeply and made her way back toward the elevators.

Door by door, she listened for a moment, then moved on. As she approached a door that stood half open, Cal thought she heard something. She stood at the door for a long moment. Then, ever so gently, she squeezed through, not touching the door, not chancing a noise from a potential squeaky hinge. She froze as she heard what seemed to be sobbing.

The sound was coming from a door just down a short hall past the office's reception desk. As she made her way along the wall, she spotted a girl with jet black hair sitting in a break room. In front of her, a pair of thick horn-rimmed glasses sat on the table. Her face was buried in her hands.

"Mei," Cal said softly, "it's time to go home."

The girl looked up and squinted at Cal. She wiped her eyes on her sleeve and put on her glasses. "Who are you?"

"My name is Cal. I'm a friend of your parents. They are very worried about you.

"I want my momma," Mei whimpered.

"It's okay, you'll be home soon." Cal smiled.

"Who are you?"

"The booming voice behind her made Cal spin around defensively.

Marco stood in the doorway like an angry bull. His territory was threatened.

"A friend," Cal said as calmly and cheerfully as she could.

"Who are you?" Marco stammered.

"My name is Cal and I have been looking for you guys. It's time for you to go home."

"This is my home," Marco said defiantly.

"No! This is a pretend home," Mei said, standing from her chair. "I want my real home."

"We can live here," Marco said, his anger turning to pleading.

"No! I want to go to my house." Mei raised both her hands and crossed her chest.

"It's OK, really. I will give you both a ride home."

"We can go home by our selfs," Marco insisted.

Cal's mind raced. She can't let them just wander off. They live in different parts of the city. She had to get them into her car and safely delivered home.

"What if I follow you to make sure you get home, OK?

"OK. But leave us alone!" Marco was showing signs of agitation.

Cal wasn't sure how far to press Marco. He transitioned from frightened and compliant to openly hostile in seconds. He wasn't her assignment, but if he became unmanageable she could have a real problem on her hands. A problem she was ill equipped to handle. He was a big kid, and being uncertain of what he was capable of doing was a bit unnerving.

"I tell you what" Cal began, "What if you guys get your stuff together and we'll all go downstairs together? That way we can be sure the door gets locked."

"I can lock the door!" Marco shouted.

"OK. OK."

Mei was sobbing softly. "I want to go home.

"You come to my house. My mom will take you home."

Marco moved to where Mei stood. He gently stroked her arm. "Are you cold?" he asked softly, "You're shaking." Marco unzipped his bright red San Francisco Forty-Niners hoodie and gave it to Mei. Without a word, she slipped her arms into the sweatshirt and zipped it up. Cal silently watched as the pair gathered their few belongings and put them in their backpacks.

"All set?" Cal asked.

There was no reply. Marco took Mei's hand and walked toward the door.

"We don't want you," Marco said not looking back.

That may well be, Cal thought, but you are not getting out of my sight for a minute.

The elevator ride was made in complete silence. Cal watched Marco in the reflection of the doors. He stared straight ahead, motionless. Mei looked down at the floor all the way to the lobby.

Outside, Marco left Mei by the door and went to the electrical box. Without saying a word or looking at Cal, Marco locked the door, returned the key, and went back to take Mei by the hand. They walked silently down the alley and to the street.

The morning fog was thick, damp, and cold. The sun struggled to burn through the moist air. Even the slight breeze that came through the canyon of buildings seemed to chill the damp air further. Visibility was cut down to less than half a block horizontally and three stories vertically. The sounds of the city were muffled and eerily quiet. The pair made their way toward the corner and the Muni Bus. Cal rolled slowly behind just within the edge of the fog.

Cal pulled up behind the bus as close as was legally permissible. Stop by stop, she watched passengers board and depart. The kids were safely crossing the city and were never more than ten yards ahead of her.

The farther from downtown they traveled, the thinner the fog became. As the bus crossed Mission the sun burst through the last wisps of fog.

Ricky woke with a stiff neck and a full bladder. He relieved himself between two cars in the parking lot across from where he had spent the night. The fog in the air was nearly as dense as the fog in his brain. He tried to smoke and drink away the visions of Trick sprawled dead across the floor; killed by the bullet he had fired. In the end he was unable to keep his eyes open and pulled over on a neighborhood side street.

His rage grew more focused and his shame was so heavy he could barely raise his head, while fragmented images of the attack on the apartment continued to swirl across this thoughts. Time and time again the door was kicked in, and his friends fell broken from the attack. He did not act, he hid. In his mind he saw his frail shaking form hiding behind a chair. Ricky was haunted by the cowardly way he had tried to shoot between the legs of chairs, instead of standing like a man and taking on the enemy man to man. He should be dead.

He returned to his car, resolute in his anger and determined to inflict damage on Norteños. They all shamed him and violated the FCBZ home turf. Ricky started the car, drank the last inch of Sloe Gin from the bottle still open in the seat next to him, and tossed it out the window. The sound of breaking glass hitting the side walk was drowned in his revved engine as he pulled from the curb.

The trip across town in the morning, foggy, rush hour traffic only added to Ricky's frustration and rage. He swore and pounded the steering wheel as the traffic slowed and came to a halt for minutes at a time. He made obscene gestures at drivers who dared try to pull into the traffic ahead of him or made maneuvers he felt slighted his dominate position on the road.

As he turned onto Mission Street, Ricky began to scour the streets for red. He was like a shark searching for the first hint of crimson in the water. The "Colors", so proudly worn as a public claim to their gang loyalty, would provide him his target. He entered the neighborhoods controlled and aligned with the Norteños and their affiliates.

Up and down the streets as far as Potrero, he circled in search of his prey. 24th, 25th and 26th streets rolled past his window with empty sidewalks. Careful not to stray into Sureño territory, Ricky nearly took a wrong turn at Jackson Park. Straying too far north could be fatal. He found it strange that the gangs claiming North and South, as their names imply, in fact, controlled the polar opposite sections of the city geographically. Empty street by empty street, his anger burned hotter with his inability to find a release for his revenge.

As he rolled through the lifting fog, he determined he would have to bring his targets out from the safety of their curtained windows and locked doors. Ricky rolled down the passenger side window. He now focused on finding one of their precious Lowrider cars. It seemed a car lowered close to the pavement, with custom paint, and sporting fancy gold spoke wheels would be easy to spot. A round racked into the chamber of his gun, Ricky went in search for the car he would fill with holes.

The sun began it flood the streets and the neighborhoods seemed to rise up through the haze. Ricky couldn't find a lowrider. He was so angry, as he reached the end of another street without a lowrider or a gangster in red, he burst into tears. He wiped his eyes with the backs of his hands and turned down 23rd street.

As he rolled down 23rd street, to his right, Ricky saw the giant XIV of gang graffiti and fired three times, his arm outstretched from his window as he passed.

"That should bring them out!" Ricky screamed.

Somewhere on I-5, Luis, Carlos, Juan, and Chuey rode along listening to music on their way home. All the anger and hatred Ricky focused on the Norteños of San Francisco and the Mission District had nothing to do with the four Mexican's from Southern California who drove north to free their friend. They had never claimed or gave the slightest indication they claimed red, Norteño allegiance, or even gang membership. Ricky just saw Brown and went to the avowed enemies of the Fire Cracker Boyz.

As he pulled through the intersection of 23rd and Shotwell, Ricky saw his target at last. Two figures, a hundred yards away, on his side of the street, walked along, their backs to him. One wore a bright red hoodie.

"They're going to die!" Ricky laughed hysterically, as he jammed down the accelerator.

The only thing blocking him was a lowered Subaru Impreza. Ricky down-shifted and passed the Subaru, barely missing an oncoming car. Fifty yards, he began to slow. His hand shook he squeezed the gun so tight.

The distance closed. Fat Mexican guy and his girlfriend, Ricky thought.

"Kiss her good-bye. Kiss her ugly ass goodbye!" he screamed, as he pulled up alongside the pair.

The thunderous blast of his automatic weapon inside the car nearly deafened Ricky. As he fired the second and third shots, the girl in the red sweatshirt spun wildly, eyes wide, gasping for air, and looking right into the car. The black bobbed hair, the thick, black-rimmed glasses; Ricky was looking into the face of his little sister, Mei. As the plate glass windows behind her shattered and fell to the sidewalk, Mei's jerking body fell into the sparkling rain of glass shards.

Ricky jumped from the still rolling car and fiercely threw his gun, hitting a car across the street. Marco was kneeling next to Mei on the sidewalk, rocking back and forth violently and screaming her name. Ricky approached and Marco stood and began swinging at Ricky, hitting him solidly in the face, neck, and chest. Ricky was no match for the size and wrath of Marco's blows. He turned and ran back to his car.

Cal slammed on her brakes, leaving a string of cars, screeching and nearly colliding, behind her. She ran from her car to where Mei lay on the sidewalk. Marcos swung at her violently. He cried, blindly swinging one second, gently stroking Mei's arm the next.

Cal knelt across from Marco and felt Mei's neck for a pulse. It was weak, but still there. Cal quickly examined Mei's thick torso for wounds. One bullet struck her rib cage, another just above her naval, and the third struck the thick part of her arm below the shoulder. Cal fumbled for her phone but her hands were too wet and slippery with blood to be able to dial.

"Call an ambulance!" Call screamed at a man standing by the car stopped behind her Subaru.

Ricky's car had rolled several lengths up the street and had come to rest against the bumper of an SUV. The alarm from the SUV added to the frantic noise and ramped up Ricky's panicked confusion. He felt his pockets for his phone, dialed three digits and waited.

"I shot her!" Ricky yelled into the phone.

"Calm down, sir. Who did you shoot?" The 911 operator asked.

"I shot her! I shot Mei. Send help, send an ambulance."

"What is your location, sir?"

"23rd Street. I don't know, uh, Shotwell. Hurry! Send an ambulance."

A crowd began to gather around Mei and Marcos. A large woman in a raincoat knelt next to Mei. She took a large blue scarf from her pocket and applied pressure to her stomach wound.

People were pointing and screaming at Ricky. Others spoke into their cell phones. Two were taking pictures of him. In the distance, the sound of approaching sirens grew louder. The swirling kaleidoscope of sounds and visuals around him, and the constant replaying of Mei's face as she fell into the sparkling waterfall of glass, was pushing Ricky to the edge of madness.

Ricky pushed his fists tight against his temples. As the owner of the SUV approached the scenes, Ricky jumped into his car and slammed it into reverse. Without looking back he floored the accelerator and disappeared into a blue haze of smoke and burning rubber.

FIFTEEN

"Lieutenant Chin on line one," Hanna said, sticking her head in Cole's door. "Nice to have you back." Her sarcasm was not lost on Cole.

"Cole, got something for you." Leonard Chin's distinctive voice carried a strange ironic tone.

"Hold on, let me grab a pencil," Cole said looking down at his tornado ravaged desk. "Ready."

"It seems once again the law of the jungle has prevailed. In spite of our best efforts to solve the Parade shooting, the answer has been dropped in our, make that, *my*, lap."

"This should be good."

"Yeah, get this. It seems a group of really ballsy Norteños kicked in the door to the Fire Cracker Boys playroom and beat the hell out of them. Slashed one with a razor blade or something, broke a couple of arms and cracked some heads, but they didn't kill anybody."

"That doesn't sound quite right." Cole smiled, knowing Chin couldn't see him.

"They didn't use guns. They beat the shit out of them with baseball bats. Even the guy that got slashed, half dozen or so cuts all across his chest and stomach and only an eighth of an inch deep."

"What about the attackers?"

"One guy shot, we don't know anything about him."

"OK, so back up. How is it we know all this?" Cole asked, not sure where this was all going.

"This is the part you won't believe. This morning I get a call from a kid named Ricky Chou. His father's on the edges of the Tongs. His kid, it turns out, is a Fire Cracker!" Chin shows an unusual outburst of excitement. "He says he's shot his sister. Two seconds later I get a call about a shooting on Shotwell. It's her, or at least it fits."

"That's not a very Chinese thing to do. I mean, to take out someone in your own family? Right?"

"Exactly. Seems she was wearing a red sweatshirt, he was out for blood and..."

"So he kills his own sister?" Cole interrupted.

"She's not dead, took three bullets, but she's still alive. She's in surgery at San Francisco General right now."

"How'd you like to live with that one?" Cole said reflectively.

"It gets weirder. This guy's either the world's dumbest criminal or world's worst shot. Get this, he shot the leader of the FCBZ! Killed him. Shot him in the back.

According to Chou, this kid they call Trick stepped in front of him. He was aiming at one of the Norteños from behind a table or something. Pow! Shoots his life-long friend."

Cole didn't respond. He couldn't. He just slumped down in his chair. No one said anything about Trick being killed. That was the cost of Anthony's freedom. A knot churned in the pit of Cole's stomach. Cole just stared at the top of his desk.

"You hear me? This kid shoots his own guy!" Chin broke the silence.

"Crazy," Cole finally said.

"Here's the part I thought you might find interesting."

"What's that?" Cole said, still reeling from Trick's death.

"It seems that the FCBZ snatched a kid off the street. Mexican kid. Held him hostage for two or three days. The *so-called* Norteños are the ones who came to rescue him. Ricky Chou says some *old guy* came looking for him." Chin paused.

"Huh, that is interesting," Cole said trying to sound calm.

"Sound like anybody you might know?"

"Not off hand," Cole replied flatly.

"This Chou kid says they both came around asking questions, lots of questions from the people in Chinatown. Said they worked for a newspaper. He was a bit fuzzy on which one."

"What kind of questions?"

"The Parade Shootings."

The silence screamed over the phone line. Chin knew. Cole knew. *First one to blink*, Cole thought.

"You been to Chinatown recently?" Lieutenant Leonard Chin was using his San Francisco Police Homicide Detective interrogator voice. Cole knew the voice.

"This old guy hurt anybody?"

"You been to Chinatown lately?"

"Did the Mexican kid hurt anybody?"

"You been to Chinatown lately?" Chin repeated.

"You know I'm reporting on the Parade, of course I've been to Chinatown. Me and half the news people in America."

"Anything I need to know?"

"Journalists as a whole, and newspaper reporters in particular, report stories like this, not make them. Have you called the *Examiner* or *The Tribune*? How about the *Mercury News*, talked to anybody there? They all have people on the street here in the City. They might know something."

"That's it? That's what you got?" Chin was obviously irritated.

"Just brainstorming. Is the Mexican kid alright?"

"I don't know."

"How's that?" Cole asked.

"I don't know who he is." It was clear to Cole. Chin didn't want to be asked that question.

"Was the sister alone?"

"No, a kid from the Mission was with her. Funny thing, a P.I. was with them. Sort of with them, she was tailing them."

"She?" Cole asked.

"Ex-SFPD, Cal Corwin. Know her?"

"Yeah, she was in my office a couple of days ago. Working on a missing person case. Did the girl show symptoms of Down Syndrome?" The picture began to come into focus for Cole.

"Both of them. Where's Anthony?" Chin fired in rapid succession.

"Asleep at my house the last I knew. He was out late with friends." Cole answered, without missing a beat.

"Are you holding back information, Sage?"

"That is a serious accusation, Lieutenant. Not something I would expect from a friend."

"It was a question, not an accusation. That wasn't a statement I would expect from someone with nothing to hide."

"If I hear anything that might help, I'll let you know. It's really sad about the girl. Is the boy OK?" Cole asked.

"Yeah. What are you doing for lunch? Talking to you has made me hungry for eel. Want to hit Okina Sushi? They make a killer Unagi Box. I'm buying," Chin offered.

"With an invitation like that you should be a writer, Chin. 12:30?"

"See you then *old newspaper guy*."

At ten-thirty Cole called Kelly's cell. "My house guest still asleep?" He asked before she could say hello.

"Nope."

"Is he sitting at the table?"

"Yep."

"He OK?"

"Seems to be."

"I'm obviously interrupting something. I'll call back later."

"Thank you for calling." Kelly ended the call.

"Cole?" Anthony asked.

"How'd you guess? He was checking on you."

"He really stuck his neck out for me. I half way wish he hadn't; then again, the other half is real glad I'm alive."

"He thinks the world of you." Kelly smiled. "You want to talk about what happened?"

"What did Cole tell you?"

"Not much. He thinks he's protecting me."

"He may be." Anthony took a sip of coffee. "I went to

get background for the parade shootings. No big deal. I know I'm a rookie, but really I was just trying to get reactions from people in the neighborhood. The Fire Cracker clowns came up and told me if I want to talk to people in their community I had to talk to somebody named Trick." Anthony took a bite of scrambled eggs. "These are really good."

Kelly smiled and took a sip of her tea.

"So, I go to this upstairs apartment with these guys. It was their hangout. It was just a bunch of guys getting loaded and hanging out. The guy in charge's name was Trick. He was really nuts. I don't know if he just smoked his brains away or what, but he was a combination of mean and just plain crazy. Anyway, I was doing my best reporter thing. A little edgy, little cool, you know the whole Sage School of Journalism thing. I whip out my recorder and Trick spots this."

Anthony puts his hand out toward Kelly to show her the faded XIV in the web between his thumb and index finger.

"I got it when I was fourteen. I was kind of a wannabe. That was it. Next thing I know I'm duct taped to a chair in a back bedroom somebody used to store junk in."

"How long were you tied up in there?"

"I'm not sure. They gave it to me pretty good." Anthony turned his head to show Kelly the side of his face. "My ribs are pretty bruised up, too. Anyway, last night I pretty much figured I was finished. I tried to make my peace with, you know, anyway, I hear all hell breaking loose down the hall. All of a sudden the door is kicked in and there is my friend Luis from L.A. I knew that it was Cole's doing."

"Cole was so worried about you he called them," Kelly offered.

"Wow. That took a lot."

"He told me at dinner that night after you disappeared. He was really conflicted. He wasn't sure unleashing their violence was the right thing to do. He said in the end all that mattered was getting you back." Kelly smiled.

"Whew."

"That's crazy, he could have gone to jail." Anthony shook his head.

"Still could, I guess. I think he just sees things differently. He would have kicked in that door himself, but knew he needed help, so he called your buddies. When they got here, they refused Cole's help." Kelly looked deep into Anthony's eyes. She decided Cole was right. He was worth saving.

"He was going to go with them? He could have gotten killed!"

"Greater love hath no man than this; that a man lay down his life for his friends." Kelly said, taking another sip of tea.

"What's that? Shakespeare?"

"The Bible."

"Has Cole got religion?"

"I think he has a lot deeper faith than we know. Let's put it that way."

Anthony took a bite of his eggs. "He has seen a lot of stuff. He's caught glimpses of the Pearly Gates more than once. I guess he figures he'd better be ready." Anthony chuckled. "He just seems a lot different than when I first met him. He's a lot, I don't know ... nicer." Anthony laughed. "Don't tell him I said that. It would be bad for his rep! I was in that room with those guys. They are a scary bunch! Cole said he was there the day before I was. He said it like it was nothing. He may be nicer but he is still a hell of a warrior."

The small auditorium of Golden Gate Academy was a churning, low roar of voices, movement, and the buzz and hum of lights and cameras. The small three-foot high stage was covered with flowers. On either side of the microphone stand, were two large, moveable corkboards covered with drawings, paintings, and handmade cards. The centerpiece of the stage was a gigantic heart with MEI in the center. Like a float from the Rose Parade, the entire thing was fashioned from crepe paper flowers and suspended by wires from the ceiling.

Cole met Anthony at the Academy for the 10:00 press conference and found a spot near the front and off to the right of the stage.

"This is quite a turn out," Anthony whispered.

"We've got it all. Gangs, handicapped kids, guy shooting his sister and best friend," Cole paused, "by accident. All we're missing is the love interest."

"Cynic," Anthony teased.

"Nope, just been here before." Cole smiled. "Have you thought of an angle for your story?"

"Story?" Anthony wasn't sure he heard correctly.

"Yeah. *My Three Days in Hell*, or *Gang Hostage: My Story*. No, no. I got it, *College Student Meets Street Gang and Survives: The Untold Story!*" Cole laughed heartily.

"Seriously, will I get to write something before I go back to school?" Anthony queried.

"I was serious. Not about the headline, but the story needs to be written, all except the escape. We'll have to work on that angle of it."

"Angle for what?" The voice that came from over their shoulders was that of Lieutenant Leonard Chin.

"The Press Conference here," Cole replied.

"You missed the Mayor and the Chief of Police. They're kind of the draw, wouldn't you think?"

"We were checking out a hot tip." Cole smiled.

"Your friend is so full of crap," Chin said to Anthony. "I know you two are up to your ass in this mess. What I want to know is the angle."

"Angle?" Anthony asked Chin but looked at Cole.

"Yeah, Mexican kid gets held by FCBZ, an old guy comes around asking questions, they both claim to work for a newspaper, some even say *The Chronicle*, and three, four, or five Norteños, or not, ride in and rescue the kid." Chin cleared his throat. "The angle would be who, and why. My people got zip from the gangbangers in the Mission. They should be bragging like mad over a stunt like this. They're quiet as can be. They actually didn't know it happened. So I figure there's an angle."

Anthony held his right hand out. "That is the angle," he said, indicating his faded tattoo. "I was a victim, held against my will. I do not intend to press charges. I would love to thank the group of concerned citizens of San Francisco who came to my aid. Sadly, they didn't leave their name and address. Cole picked me up down by The Chronicle Building and took me home. I have been asked to write the story of what happened. You'll have to read it. I'd like to know what you think."

"You teach him that?" Chin asked Cole.

"That, my friend, was 100% Anthony Perez."

"So that's that, huh."

"It would appear so." Cole grinned.

"You're a pain in the ass, Sage. If it weren't for..." Chin was interrupted by a man's voice.

"Testing, testing. One, two, three." A lanky man in dark green corduroy trousers and a denim long sleeve shirt was standing at the microphone. "Good afternoon ladies and gentlemen. Thank you for coming. My name is Thom Kyriakos, I'm a Life Skills teacher here at Golden Gate.

"The tragic shooting of one of our own yesterday is just one more of the senseless, violent acts that plague our city, state, and nation. It is our hope that, as members of the press, you show compassion and respect for our student and her family." Kyriakos turned and looked over his shoulder to the back of the stage.

"I would like to introduce Dr. Nancy Cline, our Principal, and our lead teacher, Maggie Strout."

Two women came to the front of the stage, one walking with a confident stride and the other in a wheelchair.

Taking the microphone from the stand, the older of the two women said, "Good morning, my name is Nancy Cline. I am the chief administrator here at Golden Gate Academy. First off, I would like to thank the Mayor and The Chief of Police for speaking so eloquently to the problem of youth violence in our city. Here at Golden gate we have suffered a heartbreaking loss of innocence. When you think of gang violence and the troubled violent nature of the streets, the image of children, special needs children, does not come to mind does it?"

She spoke with authority and with a clear unwavering tone. "Mei Chou, a member of our Golden Gate family, has been senselessly gunned down, and her friend Marco Gutiérrez, is left unable to understand why this happened on a street in his own neighborhood.

Her crime? She wore the wrong color sweatshirt, a sweatshirt representing our own San Francisco Forty-Niners." Ms. Cline let her statement hang in the air for a long moment.

"We are here today to speak on behalf of Mei, the children of San Francisco, and the children of America. It is not just the job of the Police. We who love children, as a parent, as a teacher, as a concerned member of our neighborhood or community, must strive to teach respect and love for all people. Race, sex, or the foolish affiliation to a color or scrap of fabric can't be the determination of the value of a life. We must stop this insanity!" Cline stepped back and handed the microphone to the woman in the wheelchair.

"Hi, I'm Maggie. I have spent my life working with these wonderful, very special children. Mei and Marco are very dear to my heart. I have watched them grow, learn, and mature. As seniors in our high school program, they were about to graduate to our adult work training program. Now my dear, sweet, Mei lays in a hospital bed clinging to life." Maggie Strout's voice cracked and she wept quietly. The room fell into a reverent silence. Maggie wiped her eyes and looked out over the audience. "I want you to meet a young man that has suffered in a way no child should. He also has seen someone he loves get shot. He is a wonderful, kind, and generous boy. He is special, you see, he has something the rest of us don't have, a forty-seventh chromosome. Marco, will you join me?"

The room burst into spontaneous applause, as Marco came from the wings to join his teacher on stage. Maggie Strout reached out and took his hand and smiled up at him. She said something the crowd couldn't hear. Marco took the microphone and walked out to the edge of the stage.

"Hi."

Several members of the audience returned the greeting.

Cole leaned over to Anthony and whispered, "I know that kid!"

"I like nice people. Mei is nice. She got shot. That is really bad." Marco looked down at the front of his shirt. "I got her blood on me. We should all be nice and not shoot people." He turned and looked back at Maggie Strout. She nodded for him to go on.

"I want kids to be safe. Gangs need to stop shooting people. Please stop!" Marco turned and walked back to where Maggie waited for him.

"We all know what the problem is and we all know love is the answer. Please tell your viewers, your listeners, your readers to consider the innocent, be they child or adult. Please help put an end to this blight on our city. Thank you for coming. We will be giving tours of our school in a few minutes, if you anyone is interested."

Cole walked toward the stage. Dr. Cline was already exiting the stage on the left side. Marco was obviously being praised by his teacher. Mr. Kyriakos was busy winding up the microphone cable. Cole was about six feet from the stage when Marco looked down at him.

A frown crossed the boy's brow and Cole could see he was trying to process a memory. As he approached the stage, he made a heart shape with his thumbs and index fingers and held it out to Marco.

"I love you too! I love you too!" Marco's face lit up with delight at the recognition of the man from the taxi just a few days before.

"Hi buddy!" Cole called out.

Maggie Strout looked from Marco to Cole completely baffled by the exchange.

"Mrs. Strout, it's him! It's him. The man, the man! He said 'I love you too!'"Marco was nearly jumping up and down with excitement.

Cole hopped up on the stage and made his way to Marco and his teacher. Three feet from them, Marco rushed forward and put Cole in a bear hug. To Cole's amazement, the boy lifted him off the ground and spun him around.

"Whoa!" Cole laughed in shock at Marco's exuberance.

"Marco! Maybe your friend doesn't like to be spun about!" Maggie Strout said firmly but happily.

Marco set Cole down and clapped his hands in delight.

"Perhaps I should explain," Cole said to Maggie. "I'm Cole Sage." Cole offered his hand.

"From *The Chronicle*?"

"That's me. This young man and I made a connection the other day. I was in a taxi when his school bus pulled up next to me. He made that heart sign and said 'I love you' through the glass. I said 'I love you too!' I guess that makes us friends." Cole laughed.

"I'm Marco," the boy said, taking Cole's hand and pumping it vigorously. That not being enough to satisfy Marco's thrill of seeing Cole, he gave him a bear hug and lifted him off the ground. Then put Cole down with a thud.

"My name is Cole. That's my friend Anthony," Cole said panting and pointing into the dispersing crowd, remembering he left Anthony without explanation.

"Hi, Anthony!" Marco yelled.

Anthony waved and started toward the stage.

"Well, Mr. Sage, you certainly made an impression." Maggie smiled.

"I couldn't leave without saying hello, the opportunity was just too good to pass up."

"I hope you will be doing a piece about our dear, sweet Mei."

"Actually, I have been working on an article about the Parade shootings. Anthony there, has been assigned the job of telling the story and its various connections," Cole replied.

"What a terrible way for the community to learn about our school."

"I tell you what. How about I come back in a week or so and talk to you about your work here?" Cole offered.

"Truly? That would be wonderful!" Maggie said, excitedly taking Cole's hand again.

"Then it's a date." Cole turned back to Marco," I hope you will tell your story to my friend Anthony when he comes to talk to you."

"Does he like kids like me?" Marco said quietly, while looking down at Anthony.

"Oh, yes," Cole said in a little too loud secretive whisper.

"Anthony, you come and talk to me!" Marco shouted.

"I'll do that!" Anthony called back.

"OK, I have got to get back to work. I'll see you again sometime, Marco." Cole patted Marco on the back and hopped down from the stage next to Anthony.

As the pair made their way to the exit, Anthony asked, "What was that all about?"

"You're never going to believe it," Cole said, turning and giving a big wave to Marco who was still watching and waving at them.

SIXTEEN

"Knock, Knock."

Cole looked up to see California Corwin standing in his doorway.

"Your secretary doesn't seem to be in," Cal stammered like a school girl. "Have you got a minute?"

"Just barely, I'm off to do an airport run. It's been a while. What's going on?" Cole said, logging off his computer.

"I wanted to thank you for leaving my name out of the article you did about Mei Chou's shooting."

"You seemed to have really, how can I put this nicely, screwed up big time. It didn't seem like it would help anybody to name names. I figured your start-up business probably wouldn't survive the hit. Besides, who doesn't mess up every now and again, right? Usually the clients don't get shot though." Cole wasn't about to let her off easy.

"Well, thank you."

"Life's all about second chances, right?

Cal fumed. She beat herself up a lot worse than that, but somehow, coming from Cole, it hurt a lot worse. She desperately wanted to impress him. She couldn't put her finger on it, but there was just something about him that reached places that hadn't been reached in a long time. And she liked it.

"I was wondering," Cal could feel the redness creeping up her neck that would soon splotch her cheeks. Her scar throbbed. "I was wondering if I could take you for a drink sometime."

"Don't drink," Cole said standing.

Just shoot me, Cal thought. "Well, maybe dinner." She felt like her tongue was shot full of Novocaine.

"That's very kind, but totally unnecessary," Cole said, grabbing his jacket off the back of his chair.

"I'm back. Any last minute orders, Chief?" Hanna called from her desk.

"Just see if you can get that guy at the art gallery lined up," Cole called back. "Now there's somebody that could use a private eye!" Cole stopped and looked directly at Cal for the first time.

"How's that?"

"This poor guy had a bunch of paintings his gallery replaced with copies. The stuff is all so weird he didn't notice until one of the artist's friends bought one. Then the artist saw it! He blew his top. Kinda funny in a way, don't you think?" Cole grinned at Cal.

Give a girl a break would ya, Cal's mind raced. *How am I going to get a date with this guy*? "Are you seeing anyone?" Cal blurted out. *Oh my God. What have I said!*

"As a matter of fact, I am. She's on her way here. Why?

Looking for the lover of an unfaithful wife?" Cole laughed. Then it hit him. She was putting a move on him. Now it was his turn to turn red. "I, um, bad joke. Look, yes I have someone very special, and um, I..."

"Oh no, not for me!" Cal lied. "A friend of mine, she's uh..."

"Oh. Oh, well. Then nope, I'm all fixed up in that department. But, I'm flattered." Cole knew she had lied, but it was a nice save.

"Do you like tea?" Cole asked.

"Is that an Asian joke?" Cal scowled.

"No! I have been drinking this incredible new tea they have at a little coffee place down the street. I thought some afternoon when you're not tied up with a case we could grab a cup. It's really good." Cole's cell phone began playing *Dock of the Bay,* it was Kelly.

"That would be nice." Cal was fuming again. *No "mercy" cup of tea, thank you! Then again...* she thought. "I would love to find a new tea. Oolong gets old after a while." She tried to sound upbeat.

"Really?" Cole said, trying to get his phone out of his pocket.

"No, it's an Asian joke." Cal grimaced, knowing she should never try humor.

"Hi Kell'. Yes, I'm on my way out. I'll be down in a minute." Cole ended the call and shoved the phone into his jacket pocket. "Well, good luck. If I hear of anybody in need of your services, I'll give them your name."

"Really?"

"You bet." Cole was moving for the door. "Got to run."

Cal barely beat him out the door. "Thanks," she said as Cole swept by.

"Sorry I can't chat. I'm late."

"You? Never!" Hanna said to Cole's back. She looked at Cal and shrugged.

"See you later," Cal offered.

"Take care," Hanna said turning to answer the ringing phone, "Cole Sage's office."

Cal made her way to the elevator, too late to ride down with Cole.

Three people and two suitcases stood outside the security gate at San Francisco International airport. Kelly Mitchell and Cole Sage stood arm in arm facing Anthony Perez.

"I for one, am going to miss you!" Kelly said reflectively. "This month flew by."

Anthony grinned sheepishly. "You've been very kind, Kelly. Thank you for everything. Thank Erin and Ben too. That Indian rice thing she made was awesome. Oh yeah, and give Jenny a big hug. Tell her I won't forget her."

"You are part of the family as far as I'm concerned." Kelly smiled.

"I just wish I could have gotten more work out of him. One lousy story!" Cole smiled broadly.

"But I got a 'by line'. That should please my academic advisor," Anthony replied.

"Front page of *Local*, I didn't see that one coming." Cole smiled.

"Liar." Anthony chuckled. "Thank Mr. Waddell for me again. He was an amazing help."

"OK, maybe."

"United Flight 1209 for Chicago now boarding at Gate 66." The muffled voice from the speaker overhead announced.

"That's me," Anthony said.

"It's been good having you around. I wish it was permanent," Cole said.

"Maybe you can put a good word in for me."

"Give me a hug." Kelly said spreading her arms.

As Anthony moved back from Kelly's embrace, he faced Cole. "I just want..."

"I know," Cole offered. "I am so proud of you there are no words."

Anthony extended his hand to Cole. Cole took it and pulled his young protégé in for an embrace. "You take care."

"You too, old man." Anthony patted Cole's shoulder.

As Anthony turned toward the gate, Cole could have sworn his eyes were full of tears. Kelly and Cole waved but Anthony didn't look back.

"You know, that young man has quite a future in front of him. What do you think?" Kelly said, squeezing Cole's arm.

"I think we should talk about *our* future."

PLEASE CONSIDER THIS

If you have enjoyed *Cole Shoot* take a moment and leave a review. Readers like you are the best advertisement in the world!

COLE SAGE WILL RETURN IN ...
COLE FIRE

ABOUT THE AUTHOR

Micheal Maxwell was taught the beauty and majesty of the English language by Bob Dylan, Robertson Davies, Charles Dickens and Leonard Cohen.

Mr. Maxwell has traveled the globe, dined with politicians, rock stars and beggars. He has rubbed shoulders with priests and murderers, surgeons and drug dealers, each one giving him a part of themselves that will live again in the pages of his books.

The Cole Sage series brings to life a new kind of hero. Short on vices, long on compassion and dedication to a strong sense of making things right. As a journalist he writes with conviction and purpose. As a friend he is not afraid to bend the law a bit to help and protect those he loves.

Micheal Maxwell writes from a life of love, music, film, and literature. He lives in California with his lovely wife and traveling partner, Janet.

CPSIA information can be obtained
at www.ICGtesting.com
Printed in the USA
LVHW051531020919
629657LV00013B/1274